## Also By Nanette L. Avery

*The Colony*

*Out of the Rabbit Hutch*

*Orphan in America*

*A Curious Host*

*Sixty Jars in A Pioneer Town*

*The Fortune Teller and Other Short Works*

*Once Upon A Time Words*

*My Mother's Tattoo and Other Stories for Kids*

*First Aid for Readers*

# WHO

# WHO

*A Novel Mystery*

---

NANETTE L. AVERY

---

Who

Printed in the United States of America

ISBN (Print): 978-1-09833-469-7
ISBN (eBook): 978-1-09833-470-3

For

Mom and Dorothy

# CHAPTER 1

*Dear Madame/Sir,*

*It has come to the attention of Tilddler and Associates, that you and other injured parties of similar circumstances were victims of grievous injustices for which you paid dearly. Although we cannot redeem or salvage stolen time, our law firm intends to recoup compensation for wrongdoings placed upon you. Please accept our invitation to attend an all-expense paid weekend where we can discuss our services and commitment towards reclaiming what is rightfully yours. We maintain you will not be disappointed. If you choose to accept our offer, please call the number listed below for further instructions.*

*Best regards,*

*Hubbard Tilddler, Esq.*

\* \* \*

THE invitation lay on the desk with the other mail. It hadn't arrived early nor late; it arrived in the afternoon directly after the first pot of tea was brewed. Goldie Hildebrandt was a slight woman, and though getting along reasonably well on her husband's railroad pension, she found life could be disappointing. She had been bitter at first, but as time passed, she tried not to dwell on its frailties. She had no children; there hadn't been time. Prison does that to a person, and she often wondered if her same mistakes happened today would she have been sentenced to the maximum.

She sipped her tea and reminisced. She had been a curious child, fair-haired, light eyes, and ever-so-bold. Perhaps if her mother had been a bit stricter, she wouldn't have found herself in the predicament that stole so much of her youth. The press didn't highlight the personal side of the story; it was the wickedness that fascinated the public. The trial may have dissolved all her dreams, but it was the look on her mother's face that left her emotionally scarred.

* * *

A few days had passed since Mr. Wolfe walked up to the post office to fetch his mail. He wasn't much for going into town, so the errand twice a week was more than sufficient. Loba, his wife, always enjoyed going along, which made this outing somewhat enjoyable. But times were changing, and despite the couple's healthy diet and fresh country air, Loba was beginning to slow down. "The hips are the first to go," reminded the doctor. So, the afternoon Mr. Wolfe carried the invitation home; his wife had stayed behind.

She was loyal, the newspapers said even to a fault, and to this day, Loba never believed her husband received a fair trial. The jury was biased, tainted with prejudice and circumstantial evidence. The victim, a sickly grandmother, further corrupted his chances of an innocent verdict. It was only by luck and sloppy police work that even now, the whereabouts of the body remain a mystery, all of which saved Mr. Wolfe from a lifetime behind bars.

\* \* \*

Norman was the biggest baby the town had ever seen. "He's the size of a watermelon!" gasped the midwife. Dr. Francois had been away treating another patient in the next village, and upon his return, declared the infant the largest the town had ever recorded. At first, Norman was considered a cute little tyke; however, his growing spurts were so quick and so unpredictable that he soon became the brunt of the town's jokes. This hefty toddler was turning into an enormous child. Soon anything that went wrong was blamed on Norman. If vegetables were missing from the gardens, the town's children would tattle on him. If a chicken got out of the coup, the fault lay on Norman. Broken toys, fights on the playground, any infractions were all blamed on the super-sized child. And as time grew, so did Norman until he stood at over 6 feet 8 inches and confirmed by the doctor as "a giant." His young adult life saw little change while his behemoth size accompanied an undeserving reputation as lazy and dolt-like. Such an unfair characterization followed him unjustly when a cunning neighbor, Jack Spriggins, framed him for grand larceny. So it was that Norman began his jail sentence as a fair-haired young man and paroled as a greying middle-aged man. Prison changed his appearance, but it also changed his opinion of justice.

When Norman received his invitation, he looked over the envelope several times and even shook it to his ear. He was not in the habit of receiving mail, and for several minutes, he wasn't sure if he cared to open it.

\* \* \*

Each recipient received the same note. None returned the call right away except Mrs. Hildebrandt, who had not been away on holiday for many years. Her instructions were to take the midday train on Friday and get off at Hillbury, the last station on its route. From there, she would take the ferry across the sound. Here she would be greeted by the lighthouse keeper, Mr. Jay, and driven by way of a coach to the mountainside lodging.

Mrs. Hildebrandt scribbled the information down on a piece of paper and read it over. At first, it seemed more trouble than it was worth, so she slipped it into the desk drawer until she pulled the calendar towards her. There was more than enough time to make a decision, but what does one wear? She mulled over her wardrobe and decided that it was almost summer, so it would be entirely suitable to wear white. But then, perhaps white would not do. A linen suit would undoubtedly show any speck of dirt, and sitting for so many hours would surely give the fabric too many wrinkles. No, the white linen was a poor choice. Her blue shirtwaist would be much more travel friendly. She opened the drawer again and decided to call back. She would leave her name and say she was attending.

\* \* \*

Norman was not in the mood to travel. He had grown weary of life's disappointments and explained away the invitation as a fast shuffle. On the other hand, there was one useful take away from the offer he couldn't dismiss. Tilddler recognized the injustices against him and was taking an interest in the messy affair. Only a law firm would invest their time, especially if there were an opportunity to make money with multiple claimants.

Norman called the number. He decided he had little to lose.

\* \* \*

Mr. Wolfe did not open his invitation; instead, it was his wife, and when she read it, she didn't bother to discuss it with him. She had made up her mind; he was going.

\* \* \*

The train to Hillbury arrived at the station on time, but Mrs. Hildebrandt did not. She was not in the habit of being on a schedule, and when the cab arrived, she was still finishing her tea. The driver, a timeworn man with an agreeable disposition, was also not in a hurry and took his time loading her bags into the trunk of his car. When both were ready, he helped her into the backseat, where she settled into the corner. And, like a pair of Sunday drivers, they chatted about the weather and the sights along the way. When there was nothing new to talk about, they started over. It had been some time since Goldie had ridden in a car, and she was feeling quite content.

Mr. Brooks was a conscientious driver, and she told him so when they arrived at the station and waited until a porter offered to help with her bags. Had it not been for a dignitary taking the same train, the baggage handler stated, it would have left ten minutes ago. The traveler found this to be a lucky sign. With someone of such importance also on board, it made her all the more giddy. "Who is it?" she wanted to know.

"As much as we've been told," whispered the porter, "an emissary and his entourage. Never seen so many bags just for one man."

"I suppose ambassadors don't travel light." She made a sour face and assumed a sudden dislike for whoever it was. "They're all the same," she mused, "thinking they're better than the rest of us. As soon as I settle into my compartment, I'll find a cup of tea."

\* \* \*

The dining car was not full, and although it was nearing 4 o'clock, not everyone practiced the tradition of teatime. "Such a lovely ritual has seen better times," she muttered overhearing the woman at the adjacent table order coffee.

She tilted her head towards the window and glared at the landscape of grey rowhouses and telephone poles taking up most of the panorama. Clotheslines of pinned sheets and streets lined with parked cars followed the train, making the expression of her mouth pout downward. "Your tea, extra lemon on the side, and honey." The waiter placed the teapot and teacup on the table, offered her a napkin, and quickly padded away. His rushed demeanor compelled her to follow his silhouette to a private table. The waiter bowed slightly at the waist and handed a menu to a thin, bearded gentleman wearing a strange-looking hat. Three younger men, each sporting a mustache, sat down at a table behind him. At once, the dining car became lively with chatter. It was apparent that the ambassador was present.

Mrs. Hildebrandt sipped her tea as she wondered what all the fuss was about. He wasn't anything particularly special, except for that hat. "And you would think he would take it off in the dining car," she scorned to herself. She lowered her eyes and watched as the waiter brought him a plate of pastries and a cup and saucer. Several indecisive moments were spent waiting for the emissary to vacillate over the platter; until finally, he selected an apricot filled pastry and a lemon curd. He folded the napkin on his lap and then, using a knife and fork, cut the pastries into smaller mouth size pieces. Each bite was relished with a slight groan of approval, all of which Goldie found quite annoying. "What's in the cup?" she asked the waiter as he poured her more tea. He looked at her with questioning eyes until she pointed with her chin towards the man.

"Hot chocolate."

"You don't say," she remarked.

"More lemon?"

"No, I'm quite fine, thank you."

The waiter slipped from table to table, nodding with great approval, and flashing his sparkling smile. Goldie screwed up her nose with the thought of cocoa and watched the emissary pat his mouth and toss the napkin aside. The three men, as if on cue, stood up and waited while the ambassador straightened his hat and moved slowly away. Then two followed several paces behind as the third gentleman removed his pocketbook and lay several bills on the table. Goldie glanced about as the entourage filed out of the car like tin soldiers. She twisted around for the waiter, but he was busy serving a table of six at the far end of the car. Having drained the last of the teapot, Goldie swirled a teaspoon of sugar around the bottom of the cup before enjoying the last swallow. A nap before dinner would be nice, she thought and dipped into her change purse and counted out a few coins, stacking them on the tablecloth.

The coffee drinker at the next table had already left, and it remained unoccupied. "I wonder if her view was any better than mine?" Mrs. Hildebrandt wondered as she took her time towards the exit. She stopped at the emissary's table and eyed his empty cup and plate. She imagined how shocked people would be if they knew a man of his distinction drank coco like a child. She laughed to herself, and then, she reached over and snatched the bills off the table, crumpling them up in her gloved palm. "Old habits die hard," and wholly detached from the rest of the car, Goldie faced straight forward, sighed contently, and walked out.

# CHAPTER 2

"I've done many things in my life, but going to the top of a lighthouse is one I've missed." Norman straddled his suitcase between his legs as he spoke. The keeper leaned his head up towards the sky and then back again, setting his chin in motion with a nod of understanding. "I know what you're thinking. A man of my size couldn't get up and around the stairwell. But you'd be surprised what I can do. I was quite athletic in my day." He patted his stomach and grinned. "Maybe more out of shape now but still, quite agile when I need to be."

The lighthouse keeper sighed. "I hadn't paid much attention to your size, but now that you brought it up, you are a big fellah."

"A giant."

"Giant?"

"Yeah, I've been called a giant so many times that I sometimes forget my real name."

"And that would be?"

"Norman."

A cool breeze blowing off the water seemed to lighten the moment. The lighthouse keeper, a crusty man with a day-old beard, appeared more annoyed about having been taken away from his usual chores. He walked with a slight limp, and though riddled with arthritis, he was careful not to complain lest a younger and more fit man was to take his place. "Please to make your acquaintance. I'm Jay."

"Perhaps when I return, you might take me up?"

"Perhaps."

A face at the window disappeared just as Norman glanced up at the magnificent structure. He wasn't ordinarily superstitious, but as he followed the old keeper down a path to the coach, he began to sense something was amiss.

\* \* \*

Wolfe was outraged that his wife had taken it upon herself to make the arrangements without his knowledge. But as always, his bark was bigger than his bite, and when she dropped him off at the station, he had calmed down. He didn't like to travel far from home; he was a creature of habit, enjoying his meals at the same time, and taking evening walks around the same park he had done for years. But after brooding and then quiet contemplation, he couldn't find any real fault in following up with what this Esquire had to say. Everything in the weekend was included, there was no outlay of money, and a few days of relaxation among others who had endured similar adversities would do him good. That's what Loba said after she kissed him goodbye and drove away.

He offered his bag to the porter and hoped his wife had remembered to pack his red ascot. "A hell of a time to think about that," he thought as he stepped up into the train. He followed the conductor into his car and tried to ignore the feeling someone was staring at him. From a side glance, he noticed an elderly woman duck inside her compartment as he approached. All the males in his family had the same effect on people, and since he had inherited their strong jawline, long pointy nose, and deep-set black eyes, assumed it was because of his appearance. He wasn't ugly, just gruff looking. And for that reason, he found it difficult to make friends. The conductor stood in the doorway as Wolfe pulled the window shade down to avoid platform loiterers from looking in. "After we get going, the dining car will be open," the trainman said.

"Thank you, but I prefer to have my dinner served here. If that's okay?"

"Certainly, Sir. I'll have someone come around to take your order."

Wolfe smiled back his approval, which appeared to have triggered the conductor's hasty retreat. Loba often warned him that sometimes his smile showed a bit too many teeth. "Next time I'll just grin," he thought.

\* \* \*

The ride to the manor house was out of a fairy tale; a vintage coach pulled by two harnessed horses steadily climbed the inclined road. The coachman mumbled and grumbled as he tried to swat away the flies with a handkerchief. His was a meager attempt at discouraging the pesky insects. Mrs. Hildebrandt felt no ill effects of the bumpy ride, enjoying the plush interior and a basket generous with snacks. She set the cloth napkin on her lap and fingered the scones as she decided which one to eat first. "Scones," she thought, "I haven't had these since before prison." Such an unpleasant reminder made her snarl.

It had been a long day of travel, and as she brushed the few crumbs off her dress, she hoped they would arrive soon. She peered out the small window and smiled. It certainly was a lovely view, for as the horses lumbered upward, the seascape grew smaller, and the land around her became more lush. It made her reminisce about her child-hood; it never occurred to her until she was older that growing up in the woods was considered out of the norm. It all seemed perfectly natural, the cottage, the picket fence, and the animals: rabbits, squir-rels, hawks, deer, and of course, bears. Mrs. Hildebrandt closed her eyes, and then, in a matter of what seemed only a moment, she heard the driver fiddling with the coach door. A pungent odor of manure penetrated her nose just as she heard him say, "We're here, Ma'am."

\* \* \*

She slowly trailed the coachman's steps up to the house, a large brick building overlooking the sound. He set the suitcase down on the front stoop. "If you don't mind, I'll leave you here now," he said. He had a crooked mouth and appeared to lean to the left, favoring that side of his body. "Maybe it's because he carries so many heavy bags with his left hand," Mrs. Hildebrandt thought as she watched him totter back to the coach and lift himself to the top of the cab. She tried to decipher how old he was, but to Goldie, everyone seemed younger than her. The oak door, sturdy and rustic, presented a large brass knocker. She peered at the doorframe, hoping for a doorbell, but there was none. She stood for several moments and backed away from the portico to reassess her position. She had learned to be leery of unlocked doors, which often came with false welcomes. Then she gained her courage and pulled back on the ring, striking the door with several bold raps. Almost immediately, the door opened with what seemed to be an enormous man taking up the entire entranceway.

"Mr. Tilddler?" she asked.

"No."

"Oh, well, I'm Mrs. Hildebrandt. Mr. Tilddler is expecting me."

"I'm Norman."

"Hello, Norman, are you the houseman?"

"No, a guest."

"Well, this is rather peculiar," she complained, looking around the man and into the house. "I suppose I'll come in and wait too," and tossing an exaggerated glance at her belongings, inched one bag forward with her foot. A fleeting distrust for the brassy woman swelled, and his eyes grew round as Norman deciphered her gesture as impertinent. But as he reached for the luggage set before him, the pushy woman charged ahead.

"This is all rather unconventional," Goldie exclaimed as Norman shut the door and set her bags aside. "I don't like the way this is all beginning to shake out. It would be so much better if Mr. Tilddler were here." She removed her gloves and revealing her uninhibited self, wandered through the foyer into the living room. "How'd you get in?"

"The front door was open."

"And you just walked in?"

"Yes, that's what I was told to do on the phone."

"Oh, my instructions were different. Mine said to arrive by way of coach, but nothing about entering on my own. I just assumed…"

"Someone would be here?"

"Something like that." She sat down on the sofa and settled back into the corner. She seemed to gravitate to corners. "Have you been here long?"

"Not really, maybe an hour." He sat down in the sofa chair and put his feet up on the ottoman. It was the first time all day that he felt comfortable.

"This is a very nice room in an old fashion kind of way."

"If you don't mind me asking, but do we know each other? You seem so familiar."

"So that's why you were staring at me. I was beginning to think I had something in my teeth. Come here closer to the lamp; my eyesight is not what it once was." The giant obeyed and leaned his face toward the light. "Hmmm, maybe, ever been to Kingston?"

"Jamaica?"

"No, New York."

"Can't say I have."

Goldie put her finger to her temple and tapped. "I know! The newspaper, I bet it was a picture in the paper."

Norman laughed, "Newspaper? Imagine my mug in the newspaper."

"Perhaps, not," agreed Goldie airing her doubts. "But sooner or later, it'll come to me."

\* \* \*

When Mr. Wolfe arrived, he could not help but to be impressed. He asked the coachman to let him off before entering through the gates. The walk would give him time to get the kinks out of his stiff legs; he told the driver. At first, there was some resistance; instructions were to drive the guests directly to the walkway. However, Wolfe's sinister appearance must have made the driver think twice and let him out without any more appeals from the passenger.

It was a narrow road, and so the coachman continued along until he found a sizable tract where the horses walked around a stand of trees, like a merry go round, and changed directions back from where they came. Mr. Wolfe waved as they passed him by and turned his attention to the tranquil surroundings. He could see the house in the distance, a large two-story square structure covered in ornamental ivy. Four fluted columns, two on either side of the door, supported an elongated overhang and encased the oak door. The residence's surroundings were well wooded, a feature that made Wolfe feel more at home.

Mr. Wolfe had been the first to arrive, greeted by a younger man in a white uniform of pleated slacks and a severely starched linen shirt. And although the houseman made no noise when he walked, Wolfe noted that it was because his feet barely touched the floor when he moved; instead, he slid. No mention had been made by Salisbury, the houseman in white, about the hostess. And as Wolfe was not much of a conversationalist, the question never arose. He was tired from his travels and the long walk with his heavy suitcase and being as there was nothing else to do, he went directly to his room where the fatigued guest lay down and promptly fell asleep.

\* \* \*

"Wolfe, is that you? Why you old son-of-a-gun!"

"Norman, Norman…no wait, don't tell me; it is you! Good Lord, how many years has it been?"

"Too damn many!" cried Norman. "You look good, really good! A little grayer than I remember, but all and all, the same."

"Thanks and you too, still big, age hasn't shortened you," Wolfe laughed. "Still tall as a ramrod. Damn, I feel awful, should have kept in touch. But you know how it is."

"Yea, I read about your case."

"Yours too." He tapped the side table and leaned back in the cushioned chair. There was a tinge of sorrow in his voice as he quickly recreated the events.

"So, you got an invitation too." Wolfe picked up his whiskey and took a sip. "Are we the only ones here?"

"No, there's an elderly woman. Mrs. Hildebrandt."

Wolfe nodded. He wasn't very good with names, but he never forgot a face. "You drinking? I can ring for Salisbury; he'll get you anything you need. Nice guy."

"Think they have a beer?"

Wolfe shrugged and wondered why the man didn't want something more expensive than beer. He could drink that at home. But then, he remembered, Norman was a simple kind of guy.

As if the houseman had heard his name, he entered the room escorting Mrs. Hildebrandt carrying a wood-handled bag over her arm that was almost as large as she was. "Mr. Wolfe, I don't believe you have met Mrs. Hildebrandt. She arrived several hours after you."

She waved her hand for them not to stand and nestled into an armchair like a cat. "Please, call me Goldie. We'll be trapped here together all weekend, so we might as well forget the formalities." She looked past the guests and turned to the Salisbury. "Can you bring me a cup of tea with lemon?"

"And a lager for me," added Norman.

"Tea and a lager, and you, Sir?" He repeated the requests and turned to Wolfe, "are you content?"

"Quite."

The three guests sat in silence as Salisbury slid out of the room. Mrs. Hildebrandt slipped her embroidery out of a canvas bag and began to rethread a needle. Norman sat with his eyes closed, but Wolfe remained slightly on edge. He sipped his drink and stared at the old woman sitting in front of him. "Goldie, Goldie, damn, I'm sure we know each other," Wolfe remarked.

"We're both from the same side of town; only I'm a bit older than you."

He continued to roll her name around in his head, annoyed that this elder was playing him. "I give up," he started to say when suddenly he sat up in his chair. "Son of a bitch! You're Goldie…!"

"The one and only." She smiled and then acting coy, retreated to her needlework.

"It seems as though our host has purposely put us together on the same collision course," Norman surmised. "Since we all have a bit of notoriety."

"Shameless, isn't it?" Goldie teased. "But, at least we know some of the players."

\* \* \*

When the three guests entered the spacious dining room, an unembellished woman wearing a red velvet dress and lace collar was seated at the head. She was neither attractive nor plain, perhaps striking would be the best adjective for her looks. And no one would know that she had difficulty walking had there not been a white-handled cane leaning against the table. "Please forgive me for not being here when you all arrived, but my train was delayed by inclement weather. It appears that the storm I rode through has not yet arrived." She smiled and floated her hand above the chair next to her. Mr. Wolfe, if you would sit to my left, Norman, to my right, and Mrs. Hildebrandt, why don't you take the seat opposing mine. When the others arrive tomorrow morning, I will have the butler add additional leaves to the table. In the meantime, we can have a cozy dinner. I do hope you like lamb." She waited as they made audible noises of pleasure at the announcement of lamb, and after pulling out chairs, while Salisbury helped Goldie, all were sitting attentively like children in a classroom waiting for the teacher to speak. All eyes were on the woman in red.

Salisbury returned with a bottle of Malbec and poured a small amount into the hostess's glass. After taking a sip, she returned a look of approval. He slid along the floor and poured wine into the other glasses. "I hope you all are finding your accommodations comfortable," she said, raising her glass. "Here's to a successful weekend!"

"To a successful weekend," they chanted, all except Mr. Wolfe.

"If you don't mind, but I am a bit curious. Who are you?" he asked the bubbly woman.

"Oh, silly me, of course, we haven't been formally introduced. I am Tamaya Rosebud. A librarian."

"A very honorable career indeed," piped in Mrs. Hildebrandt, who was enjoying her wine perhaps a bit too much, for already her glass was almost empty.

"And if you don't mind me asking, just what is your connection with this whole event?" asked Wolfe, ignoring the older guest's giddiness.

"It is I who arranged our meeting. My attorney, Mr. Tilddler, sent your invitations. I didn't think you'd come if you received one from a librarian."

"Probably not," agreed Norman with a note of wariness in his attitude.

But it was the smell of dinner that began to lighten the mood as Ms. Rosebud, elated by Salisbury's perfect timing by carrying a tray of roast lamb with mint sauce into the dining room. "Oh, let's not ruin our digestion with a lot of business talk," bubbled the librarian. "I want you to enjoy your meal, and after dinner, we can get to small talk."

"Bon appetite!" cried Mrs. Hildebrandt. She had decided that if Norman and Wolfe wanted to be a pair of spoiled sports, let them. As for her, she was going to milk this weekend for all it was worth.

# CHAPTER 3

"A great deal of planning went into this living room," remarked Norman. He was awestruck by the fineries around him, along with feeling a bit out of sorts, having surrendered to the straight back chair. A few extra seats had been brought in from the dining room to accommodate the arriving guests.

"Oh, do sit on this comfy sofa," Mrs. Hildebrandt said, tapping the cushion. After eating such a big meal, she was feeling quite content. But Norman did not take the invitation to move and remained where he was lest his great weight would cause a see-saw effect, causing the plush sofa cushion to plunge like a deflated balloon.

The fireplace with its white marble mantle was the focal point of the room. Cattycorner, a pair of French doors opened to the veranda that wrapped around the entire rear of the house. Four windows draped in floor-length brocade exposed either the sunlight or moonlight, depending upon the time of day. On the opposite wall stood a sideboard and mahogany bookshelf. In the far corner, a miniature grand piano poised like an awkward child.

"Do you play?" Norman asked, pointing to the piano.

"Not well, but I do a great rendition of *Mary had a little lamb*," Ms. Rosebud chuckled, but no one else in the room seemed to find her joke funny.

Mr. Wolfe picked up his demitasse and brought it to his nose. It had a wonderful aroma, and it made him almost drowsy. He turned to the hostess and smiled, but remembering what his wife said, he toned his expression down to a grin. "Tell us exactly why you have gone to such great lengths to gather us here." He had grown especially tired being as he was in the habit of taking naps during the day. It was time she gave them some answers.

But the calm of the evening was suddenly interrupted by a great rumbling, followed by a flash of lightning that cut like a blade. The wind clawed down the chimney, and then it began to rain. "I believe this is the tenth anniversary of the great flood. But don't worry; we get rainstorms like this all the time," Ms. Rosebud remarked. "I do hope it doesn't prevent the next group from arriving, though," she muttered under her breath. She looked at her watch and then turned back to her guests. "It all started when I read an article in one of my library journals about Morgan Babbitt Publishing Company. There is often a write-up about a successful entrepreneur. Well, anyway, it got me thinking about their books, and how many of them are my favorites." Norman turned to Mr. Wolfe and shrugged. She pulled the cane towards her and slowly made her way up out of the chair to the breakfront, where she opened the drawer and removed a dog-eared magazine. "I've been saving it for just this moment." She shuffled through the yellowing pages until she came to one that made her clear her throat before reading aloud.

*Morgan Bobbitt Publishers was launched in 1923 by a Swiss émigré, Almond Renoir, publishing fictional novels and handsomely designed editions of classics, anthologies, and fairy tales, for which he commissioned a studio of full-time illustrators. After his death in 1951, Renoir's widow, Francesca Cosse Renoir, took control of the business in addition to perpetuating her passion as a collector of children's literature. After retiring from the company, she turned the publishing dynasty over to their children, Maurice and Evette Babbitt. The firm continued to initiate and encourage the careers of many talented authors and illustrators. However, their greatest achievement became known as the "second golden age of children's literature" by lucratively remarketing and reviving favorite classic fairytales."* Tamaya folded the article and placed it back in the drawer before returning to her chair.

"I'm afraid I don't see the point," explained Mr. Wolfe, a bit disappointed by the anticlimactic set up by Ms. Rosebud's train of thought. He sipped his demitasse and sighed.

"But I see a connection!" piped in Goldie. "Morgan Babbitt Publishers, they're the ones who have the rights to my story."

"Me too!" added Norman, who came alive with this bit of proclamation.

"And you, Mr. Wolfe?" asked the librarian.

He put his cup down and scowled. "It seems so."

"And the other guests will also confirm they too are connected. You are all part of the great publishing empire we know as Morgan Babbitt Ltd," added Ms. Rosebud.

"So, what's the point of having us here? I'm sure it's not because of our infamy," declared Wolfe.

"Infamy," pouted Goldie. "I rather like to think of it as notoriety. Look, even Ms. Rosebud is a fan of our youthful escapades."

"Well, if you ask me, I have to agree with Wolfe," nodded Norman, still appearing out of sorts in the too-small chair for the large man. "I believe most literary critics have branded us fiends, even villains."

"Precisely, my point!" the librarian gloated.

"Bastards," grumbled Mr. Wolfe sitting up in his wingback.

"I believe we have had enough chatter for one evening," the hostess suggested seeing as the discussion was not sitting well with her guest. "In the morning, after a good night's sleep and a hearty breakfast, we will rectify these wrongs."

"An excellent idea," remarked Salisbury, who had slid into the room towards Mrs. Hildebrandt. "Let me help you to your room, Madame," he said. And placing her hand on his forearm, he pulled the cranky woman to her feet.

"I hope the storm doesn't keep you all up," remarked the hostess. "I, for one, find it quite soothing."

The earlier stages of the evening were wearing off with tired affirmatives, and 'good night' salutations. Each guest went their separate way, and as the lights of the storm-filled each bedroom room, there was a volley of anticipation floating throughout the house of what the next day would bring.

* * *

Norman placed his knife under the pillow, a ritual he performed before bed ever since his release from prison. He was never going to be vulnerable again. Being big was once a curse, but he learned the hard way how to use his size to manipulate situations. The concealment of the knife was for one of those "just in case" moments. He closed his eyes, and in a matter of only a few minutes, he was asleep.

\* \* \*

Mr. Wolfe was old, but his hearing was still as keen as when he was a pup. He lay on his back and closed his eyes. He hadn't been apart from his wife since prison, and now so many miles away, he regretted this trip. He turned over on his side and pulled the pillow under his chin. His instincts told him something was not right. The storm was subsiding, and as he listened to the rain, he found himself slowly drifting off to sleep.

\* \* \*

Goldie Hildebrandt was too keyed up to sleep. She liked things in a particular order and found she couldn't go to bed until her clothes were placed in the dresser, and her dresses and blouses hung up in the closet. She arranged bottles of her homemade remedies on the bureau, and like every night before retiring, she took a teaspoon of cod liver oil. She stood in her dressing gown by the French door and peeked outside. Such a lovely room, she thought nosing about. The crystal ashtray was especially lovely, too pretty to snuff out dirty cigar butts. She set it back on the writing desk, deciding it would make a nice souvenir to take home. She pulled down the comforter and lay down between the sheets. Not too hard, not too soft, the bed was just right. And then, she also fell right off to sleep.

* * *

Mr. Stiltskin's knock was more than robust for an early morning arrival. Salisbury opened the door to the older man measuring little more than four feet tall. With white hair and a well-groomed beard, he was much like St. Nick but not quite as round. His brows were thick and bushy arching over pale blue eyes. He had a friendly appearance, and though he was not a hearty looking fellow, his demeanor was rugged for his diminutive size. "I'm here on account of the invite," he cheerfully said, and handing the houseman his duffle bag, he poked his head through the threshold.

"We've been expecting you," declared a voice from the inner sanctions of the house. Salisbury nodded and taking the cue, allowed the small fellow to enter. "I hope you're hungry because breakfast is ready," called Ms. Rosebud as Mr. Stiltskin followed the overture into the dining room. "Why don't you take a seat beside our newest guests," pointed the hostess. "You can sit between Javotte and Tisbe." The two women, not much older than Mr. Stiltskin, looked fatigued, for they had taken an earlier train, which, in their opinion, took longer than necessary. The two women, both quite ordinary in appearance, could only be sisters since not only did they have a strong family resemblance, but their mannerisms were strikingly similar. The little man took his seat and surrendered his hat to the houseman, who was quite pleased to remove the dusty article from the dining room. "I am so pleased you could all could join me. The other guests are out in the garden, and anytime now, the last of the latecomers will arrive."

"It is so hard to get everyone together these days," chimed in Tisbe. "Mother was so good at getting parties together, rest her soul."

"That she was," remarked Javotte.

Salisbury glided around the table and refreshed the empty cups with tea. "What may I get for you, Mr. Stiltskin?"

"Coffee, black and three lumps of sugar," he grinned and exposed several missing teeth, of which he was not the least bit self-conscious.

"Stiltskin, Stiltskin, the name is so familiar," mused Javotte.

"Call me, Ray; we should be on a first-name basis."

The two women giggled and nodded in unison. "And you can call us by our first names too," explained Javotte. "That's Tisbe, and I'm Javotte."

"We're sisters," they said with one voice.

However, Ray was too busy dunking his toast into his coffee and slurping his oatmeal to pay any attention to the small talk, which Ms. Rosebud took as an opportunity to draw the two ladies' focus away from the uncouth little man.

\* \* \*

Mr. Wolfe entered the dining room, wearing an expression of boredom. Mrs. Hildebrandt and Norman flanked him. They had taken a leisurely walk around the grounds and were ready for a second cup of coffee. The two sisters retired to the library, which left the hostess, and Mr. Stiltskin still seated at the table. But before any formal introductions, the small man jumped to his feet and offered an extended hand to the incoming guests. "Damn it, if this isn't the reunion of the century," he cried. "Goldie, you don't look a bit over…"

"Don't say it, Ray," she snickered and grabbing the man around his neck, they embraced. "My, you are the same scoundrel, aren't you?"

"That I am Goldie. So, I guess we're all here for the same reason," he hinted and turned to Ms. Rosebud with a glimmer of satisfaction.

"Still doing magic tricks?" Norman asked.

"Hell no, haven't done one since the fiasco with the gold bullion," sputtered Ray. "Got me into too damn much trouble. I barely got out with the shirt on my back. By the time I paid off the lawyer bills, I didn't have two nickels to rub together." Mr. Wolfe nodded with understanding.

Ms. Rosebud, ignoring the lamentations of lost time, was the only one to notice the rain. Unlike the warm and sunny day, she hoped for, her plan of serving lunch on the veranda was spoiled. She continued to debate with herself as to where they should dine when she was happily interrupted by the presence of her confidant and lawyer friend from Tilddler and Associates, Dr. Peri Cason. Trailing behind her was a neatly dressed gentleman sporting an out-of-fashion copper beard tapered to a point. "My dear old souls, you have arrived!" the hostess announced.

"I'm not sure if I should take that as a term of endearment or not," rebuked Dr. Cason. "Aside from my greying hair, I don't feel the least bit old.

"Nor I," agreed the dapper man.

"Tell me, how was your trip?"

"Too damn wet for my taste," quibbled the lawyer.

"And you, Mr. Dover?"

"Enjoyed the boat ride across the sound. Couldn't have been more invigorating."

Ms. Rosebud politely smiled as she sized up his seemingly sarcastic answer. The others, except for the two sisters, stood idly as informal introductions were exchanged. Harold Dover was the agent on behalf of the Babbitt Publishing Company, and Peri Cason was an attorney and forensic specialist. The hostess was basking in the delight that everything was going along so warmly until someone brought up the weather. As if a raincloud formed overhead, the mood suddenly turned glum.

"It's positively depressing," remarked one of the spinsters.

"Yes," nodded Goldie. "Lousy, just lousy!"

To look at the hostess, it was apparent she was disheartened, so, in the suddenly cramped quarters of this circle of guests, she did what any good hostess would do, suggest they join her in the library to play cards, checkers, or chess. At one o'clock, a buffet would be provided in the dining room, and with any luck, the sun would be shining, and they could all retreat to the veranda.

* * *

But it wasn't, and the only thing that arrived by way of the veranda for lunch was Mr. Jay wearing a yellow oilskin rain jacket and matching overalls. "Salisbury, get him a towel," cried the hostess. "My word, what brings you here in this dreadful weather!" she asked, as the rain-drenched sailor dripped water on her wood floors. "Take that thing off and come get yourself a cup of tea!" she insisted. "You don't want to catch a cold!"

"Brandy would be better suited for this occasion," said Javotte looking curiously at the man as if she had never seen anyone disrobe.

However, to her relief, or perhaps her disappointment, he was fully dressed beneath his raingear.

"I came to let you know that if anyone is thinking of leaving anytime soon, don't. The last ferry arrived with them two," he said, pointing to Dover and Cason. "The sound's kicking up, and now the boat engine's flooded. It'll take a few days to dry out." He wiped his face with the towel and tossed it back to the houseman who, in turn, threw it down in the puddle. "I hope you've got enough supplies," Jay said, emphasizing the conditions.

"How did you manage to get up the driveway?" exclaimed Ms. Rosebud ignoring his chatter.

"Pushed my bike, but the rain's coming down pretty hard and fast. I got my son, Reggie, tending to the lighthouse. If you don't mind, I'd like to wait a bit. My bicycle's parked under the overhang."

"Of course not, Mr. Jay. If you wish, join us in the library for a hand of bridge," the hostess suggested. "You do play bridge, I hope." With a half-smile that could have been interpreted as disgust, she led him to the library.

Salisbury looked at the floor and then glanced over his shoulder. His outlook on the day hadn't included mopping. The towel would take care of the wet floor, but as what to do with the man's raingear, that was a nuisance question. A soggy pile of yellow oilcloth was waiting for him and him alone. "Well, he won't need them for a while," the finicky butler muttered. And with his foot, he slid the pile across the floor, opened the door, and with a good kick, booted the whole mess out.

\* \* \*

"Ever been in jail?" Norman asked. He pushed his red checker forward and took the little man's piece.

The elder made a scowl and put his hand on his chin as if in contemplation. "Nope, just the drunk tank. No cot, no chair, just a bench, and a toilet. I had a cell to myself a few times. Once, they gave me a blanket and pillow. I think they felt sorry for me since it was Christmas." His hand hovered over his piece, and then he pulled it back.

Norman nodded but had no sympathy for his opponent's frivolous tales of woe. He'd heard everything before, and the only conversation he was interested in was what he could get out of this weekend. "So, how'd you avoid doing time?"

Ray leaned back in his chair and winked, "I turned state's evidence," he said. "Of course, it cost me plenty, everything I had stashed away, and my reputation…shot. I suppose it was worth it, but sometimes I wonder."

"You must have had a great lawyer."

"Lawyers," he said with correction. "A whole damn office full of em' that are now living off my money!" His face grimaced when he spoke. He leaned forward and whispered, "I'm a bit leery of that Cason woman, hope she's on the up and up."

Norman got a whiff of the old man's breath when he spoke and wondered if the scoundrel had raided the liquor cabinet. A bit early for a drink, but who was he to pass judgment. "States evidence?" the giant questioned, ignoring the statement about the lawyer who was at another table playing bridge.

"Somewhat of a stretch, but it stuck. I turned the table on the miller; he concocted a story that I was trying to swindle them. Now, what the hell would I want with a baby? I wasn't about to take the whole rap myself. He and that whimpering daughter could have walked away Scott free if I hadn't had enough sense to hire a private detective. Amazing what money can buy."

"Damn lucky break," agreed Norman. "Damn lucky."

"You said it!"

"Mind if I sit in and watch?" The woman grinned crookedly and, for the first time, noticed a scar on Norman's face. It wasn't big, but a ragged line that lay quietly across his brow. She pulled the chair and sat down with her hands folded on her lap.

"Looks like your sister is busy," Ray said, turning Tisbe's attention to the lighthouse keeper and Javotte engaged in a game of scrabble with Goldie. "Two's company," he laughed.

"I haven't the slightest idea what you mean!" scoffed the sister.

"Lay off," exclaimed Norman. It was apparent that Ray was enjoying his role as instigator. However, it may have been too late for Tisbe had already become aware of her sister's interest in the seaman.

"I didn't say anything!" defended Mr. Stiltskin. "Besides, aren't we all here for a little fun?"

"Personally, I am not here for entertainment. Who's winning?"

"Nobody yet," Norman explained. "You can play winners if you like."

"I could, but I can't. I don't know how to play."

"Too bad," Ray added. "Well, you sit there like a good girl and just watch."

Tisbe had little patience for the game, and while the two men quibbled over who moved what piece, she excused herself and wandered into the kitchen where Salisbury was preparing cucumber sandwiches.

"When Ms. Rosebud asked me to help this weekend, I didn't know I would be serving all day long!" he grumbled. "Never seen so many plates of food in such a short amount of time."

"Evidently, you're not accustomed to entertaining," the aggravated sister said. The gangly women reached over and pulled a red smock off the peg.

"Not for a crowd of this size," he complained. "I haven't been off my feet since the first guest arrived."

"That would have been Wolfe," Tisbe remarked and tied the sash. She rolled up her white shirtsleeves and brushed the front of her apron. "Now, may I help you with some of the preparations. I really would rather be in here than out there," she scoffed. Then realizing her faux pas began to explain. "You see, I hate to see my sister make a fool of herself."

"Fool, Madam?" inquired the houseman, who tried not to show his enthusiasm for gossip.

"It appears that my sister, Javotte, has taken to that old seaman."

"Mr. Jay? Oh, pray tell me, what makes you think so?"

"A woman can tell. She nearly fell over her own feet when he helped her off the boat yesterday. I wouldn't be surprised if he planned this whole thing."

"Planned, planned what?" Salisbury asked, handing her a cucumber to slice.

"Planned to seduce her!" she exclaimed, and with several whacks, she split the cucumber into two large chunks. "Yes, I imagine the old sea dog must know about our inheritance," she muttered.

"Inheritance?" the interested cook reiterated.

"Mother left us each a bit of money, that is after having to pay compensation to our stepsister. It would have been a fortune, but…"

"But?"

"Well, everyone knows the tale. It was all a huge misunderstanding. However, the jury didn't think so." Tisbe's tone had turned more remorseful than angry, and suddenly, she began to weep.

"Dear, dear, please, don't cry, why you'll get the sandwiches all wet. Why don't you go upstairs until you feel better? When you return, you can help me cut up the strawberries." He patted her gently on the shoulder and watched as she wiped her eyes with the back of her hand.

"You're an awfully nice houseman, Salisbury," she sniffled, handing him back her apron. "I think you're very nice. I'll be back right back."

"Thank you, Madam," he said. "I'll be here."

# CHAPTER 4

"WHAT'S the matter?" It was Dr. Cason, who first noticed the visible change in Wolfe's demeanor after the telephone call with his wife.

"My royalty check didn't clear," he gripped. "I don't suppose you know anything about it?"

"I haven't the slightest idea of what you're talking about?" answered Cason picking through her hand of cards as if it were a bouquet.

"Come and sit back down and let's finish our game," replied the hostess, trying to ease the tension. "I believe it's your turn to bid, Mr. Wolfe."

"No, it's mine," reminded the lawyer.

Wolfe stood behind Mr. Dover, his hot breath falling over the seated man. "I hope you aren't peeking," said the player. "Although it wouldn't matter since we are partners."

"If I weren't in mixed company, I'd…"

"You'd what? Do the same thing to me as you did to that poor old woman?" taunted the agent.

"You don't know what you're talking about; they never found the body!" Wolfe moved around the table, almost ghost-like.

"That's right," Dover answered coolly. He straightened up in his chair; he was enjoying himself.

"Don't take that crap from him, Wolfie!" provoked Goldie, the busybody, from across the room.

A shifting mood of hostility pierced the room, followed by, "Lunch is ready!" In the glow of the chandelier's light, those seated at the game tables rose to their feet. Wolfe extended a harsh look towards the instigator, who appeared not the least bit troubled, having declared to himself as the victor in round one. Fate looked out over the room like a mounted deer head over the mantel. Without much more banter than Ray's outrageous belch, everyone filed into the dining room where a buffet lunch was set out. Tisbe stood by the sideboard, fixed on Mr. Jay, who was standing behind her sister, making what appeared to be friendly advances. Tisbe's eyes widened as she watched Javotte giggle, undaunted by the man's shameless flirtation. Tisbe felt her cheeks flush and reluctantly turned away. A platter of deviled eggs suddenly resembled yellow eyeballs. She tried to scoop one up with the spoon, but she was too nervous, and they slipped around the plate-like fish. Her eyes burned cold as she tried to appear nonchalant, and sauntered eggless back into the library with the others. Only Ms. Rosebud waited for Salisbury to serve her.

"I believe these strawberries are worthy of an award!" exclaimed Goldie. "Everything is delicious and very dainty."

"Yes, dainty," muttered Norman picking up a crustless sandwich. "What is this?"

"Cucumber sandwich," Dover said. "Very good for the digestion too."

"I think I will take that drink now, Salisbury," said Mr. Wolfe gloomily.

"Of course, Sir. On the rocks."

The room was considerably quiet except for the slurping and finger sucking of Mr. Stiltskin. Ms. Rosebud sat with her plate of tea sandwiches on her lap while Dr. Cason attempted to console her that the day was not in ruins. A persistent pattering of raindrops fell against the panes crafting an even more somber mood.

"Look Wolfe; I think we got off on the wrong foot. I have a bad habit of rubbing people the wrong way." The agent sat down and offered his hand, but Wolfe's reluctance was inescapable as the wedge between his brows knit together. "Come on, sport, no hard feelings," coaxed Mr. Dover. "I think after this escapade is over, you'll be happy we've met." Wolfe stared him in the eye and ignoring his wife's advice, smiled widely, and shook the outstretched hand. He eased into the chair and began to pick at his cucumber sandwich as if it were rabbit food. He had met guys like Dover in prison and learned to tolerate them. The whiskey felt good going down his throat, and he was finally beginning to relax. The rain was falling even harder, muffling the light laughter coming from Javotte. She was dangling a strawberry over the sailor's mouth, and like a fish to bait, he caught it.

"You see," whispered Tisbe to the houseman. "She's shameless! I'm just so happy Mother isn't here to see her make such a fool of herself!" Salisbury smiled enviously at the old salt while Tisbe's eyes traveled around the room. No one else appeared to notice the two lovebirds. Everyone had strayed off into their private conversations. The jealous sister set a bowl of fruit on the sideboard and drifted back to the dining room. She was hungry from quarreling with herself. She pouted at how few sandwiches remained and placed the last three on her plate. A bowl of potato salad looked most unappealing; however, to her delight, the hearts of palm and artichokes had barely been touched.

Tisbe wandered over to the window with her plate and looked out. A flash of light flickered the shadow of a brown bird. She tapped her fingers against the pane, but the rain was too loud for the bird to hear her. She watched for a moment before taking a bite of her sandwich when a terrified shriek interrupted her tranquility.

"Get a doctor!" cried a desperate plea.

Tisbe thought it was her sister's voice but couldn't be sure. Then two other strained voices were raised in a prolonged cry for, "Help him up!"

"Ms. Rosebud and Goldie?" she thought. Tisbe nibbled her sandwich as several men elevated a holler of appeals.

"Water! Get some water!"

She heard the chattering of commands, and an "easy does it!" She watched from the side-lines as Norman and Mr. Dover carried a limp Mr. Jay up the stairs. A line of do-gooders followed with water. The commotion finally died down when they reached the first landing and deposited the sorry man into one of the spare bedrooms. The door shut behind.

Tisbe sighed with exhaustion. "These sandwiches need a touch more lemon juice," she thought and straining to see outside, continued to watch the rain.

\* \* \*

"It was you, wasn't it?"

"What are you talking about?"

"You gave something to Jay; I can tell when you're up to no good." Javotte followed her sister into the kitchen. "You're jealous because I was having fun, and you aren't. And now he's dead!"

"Dead!"

"Well, I think he could be dead. He's still upstairs in bed, and Dr. Cason said if he had eaten any more of those strawberries, he would be." The woman's declaration ended with a tone of indignation.

"Almost and is are two completely different things. Besides, how can you accuse me of something so heinous?" lamented Tisbe with crocodile tears. "After all the things we've been through."

"Oh, I'm sorry Tis, it's just that you are the only one who doesn't like him, that's all."

"Well, just don't go around telling people that I tried to kill the old codger, it's bad luck, you know."

Javotte nodded her head in agreement, only after having her sister promise not to call him an old codger.

* * *

No one sighed more loudly than Ms. Rosebud. There was an uninvited man in her spare bedroom and a small flood on the veranda. She knew about the latter only because water was seeping in from beneath the French doors. Salisbury had already made his rounds in each room and mopped up any water that he could see. "Don't worry, Madame," he said. "It should stop any day now." He smiled maniacally, but the hostess was too busy herding the guests into the living room to notice his bad humor.

"How's Popeye?" asked Mr. Stiltskin.

"He'll be alright," said Dr. Cason.

"What happened? One minute he was fine, and the next he turned blue and couldn't breathe," quizzed Goldie.

"To the best of my diagnosis and let me remind you I am only a forensic scientist, it was a reaction to something he ate. Allergic reactions can be deadly if not treated immediately."

"Such a shame," lamented the elder.

"Yes, such a shame," agreed Tisbe.

An hour had elapsed since the grave incident, and restlessness was now advancing among the guests. Tamaya Rosebud tapped her cane, and as if calling the court to order, she signaled everyone to find a chair. "My intentions for the weekend will now come to light," she began. "First, I want to thank all of you for traveling here on such short notice, assembling a group from so far away is a challenge. I will begin by telling you a bit about myself. As the head librarian at the Elwood Greens Division of Libraries, I am a noted authority on classical literature. I have read many versions of your tales, which I have found notably similar for the following reason. In each situation, the authors have independently, yet collectively, characterized your personalities with insensitivity. They often villainize and defame you with descriptions such as, and I quote, *'My man is an ogre, and there's nothing he likes better than boys broiled on toast. You'd better be moving on, or he'll soon be coming.'* This ogre is referring to Norman, grotesquely implicating that he eats children." Ms. Rosebud shook her head with disgust as she continued. "The authors spared no one, not even the reputation of innocent children in their stories. Here is a line that always sticks in my throat when I read it. *'She could not have been a good, honest little girl; for first she looked in at the window, and then she peeped in at the keyhole and seeing nobody in the house, she lifted the latch.'* This infamous scene refers to Goldie when she came upon the house in the woods." Ms. Rosebud turned to the two sisters, hoping they would not be too offended with the detailed excerpts about them. But the youngest of the two interrupted Tamaya before she spoke.

"Let me tell everyone that may have forgotten a few of the cruel remarks written about us; these words I have condemned ever since the first day I read them!" seethed Javotte. *'They were fair in face but foul at heart...'* And remember this one, Tisbe, *'a widow, (that's Mother), with two hard-featured daughters, was very proud and overbearing; and, if her two daughters had only never been born, or, being born, had died, she would then have possessed the vilest temper in all the world. As it was, the three were all equally gifted in that respect.'"* Ms. Javotte pulled a handkerchief from her pocket and wiped her brow. She was shaking, and her sister called for Salisbury to bring them both a brandy to calm their nerves.

A climate of resentment circled the room as Ms. Rosebud spoke. Mr. Dover, pulling on his beard, sat stiff as a corpse. Even though he had not personally taken the pen and written the stories himself, he grimly felt blame sliding off the tongues of this strange group of characters. It was in his interest to temper the situation.

"It's my turn!" squealed Mr. Stiltskin. "And brother, do I have a story."

"Everyone knows it, Ray," said Wolfe with boredom. "After all, your name is synonymous with kidnapper."

"My point exactly! But it's all lies. I was cleared fair and square. But those authors, they tarnished my image; they made me loathsome!"

"And you, Mr. Wolfe, do you wish to add anything?" asked the lawyer.

"Add anything to this therapy group? I don't go in for feel-good sessions. I don't have anything to say that nobody doesn't already know."

"Then you don't mind if I point out the constant harassment you and your family have endured for centuries. I know that it goes all the back to antiquity," Tamaya stressed.

"Go ahead," he shrugged. "But they've heard it all before."

"These excerpts cited from several books deem Wolfe as evil and heartless. I quote, '*Mr. Wolfe. He is no friend of ours, and you must not talk with him, for he is cruel and will do you harm.*' And then there is this infamous and monstrous rumor precipitated by the earliest edition and repeated all too often. '*You must be very careful while I am away. If wicked Wolfe should get in, he would certainly eat you.*' "

Open mouths, pouting lips, silent-movie style, all were mute; even Ray Stiltskin didn't utter a word. Ms. Rosebud continued. "I contacted other victims, but in some cases, the invitations came back marked return to sender. Some were undeliverable." The dreary weather imparted to the afternoon a moroseness reminiscent of hearing bad news. There was no mistaking that the day was shedding despair, an exactly opposite effect the hostess had intended. "Salisbury," said Tamaya, "please get everyone a drink, I think we could all use one. I know I do." His starched white uniform appeared to be the only bright spot in the room.

"Would brandy be acceptable?" he hoped. The houseman wanted nothing more to do than to fill each glass with the same drink.

"Certainly, that will be fine." And with an affirmative nod, he quickly glided away before she could give the next order.

"So," said Dr. Cason tapping her fountain pen on a pad. She liked to take notes when she talked. "I believe we need to get to the heart of why we asked you all here."

"Finally," muttered Javotte under her breath.

"It is obvious that you have all been maligned and defamed by the authors who have written your tales. Then, to make matters even more sordid, for decades, they have passed through the hands of different publishers without concern for any of you. Ms. Rosebud has been following your lives and amassed a sizeable collection of books with your stories. And though she cannot give many of you back the years lost in prison or personal exile, she believes it is time for monetary retribution."

Dr. Cason paused to look down at her notes just as Salisbury entered with several uncorked bottles of brandy. "I assume everyone would like some spirits," he asked.

"Lord, yes!" exclaimed Goldie.

"Brandy all around," squealed Ray with his usual zealous banter.

It took several minutes for each glass to be filled and several more minutes for everyone to get settled again. The brandy was regarded as a positive improvement, one that was summed up as 'necessary.' "Madame, I'm going to check on our upstairs guest," said Salisbury, making his appearance known.

"Thank you, Salisbury," and with a light dusting of her hand, shooed the man away like a pesky fly.

"We were discussing retribution." Peri Cason looked around the room with a changed attitude towards the serious. "This is where

Mr. Dover fits in. We see that all of your copyrights are with Babbitt Publishing, and to date, they continue to publish and distribute your stories."

"If you don't mind, I would like to say something before you get too far along," interrupted Norman. Today he chose to sit on the sofa, where his knees were bent almost up to his shoulders. Feather pillows were his nemesis. "We are all too familiar with the Babbit's tactics since they distribute our royalty checks." He then turned to look around and noticed everyone was wagging their heads in agreement.

"Except mine bounced!" grumbled Wolfe.

"I think I can explain. That wasn't supposed to happen," Mr. Dover lifted his drink and took a sip after he spoke. He'd be damned if he was going to apologize for the accounting department.

"Damn right!" barked Wolfe.

"Gentlemen, please," scoffed the youngest sister. "I want to hear about this monetary thing."

"Me too!" snapped the little man who was looking around for Salisbury to pour him another round.

Harold Dover had the feeling this wasn't going to be easy. He had gotten their attention and hoped there wouldn't be any more interruptions until he finished with what he had come to say. "I have been instructed to offer each of you a full year's compensation package in addition to the release of all publication rights. Babbitt Publishing has agreed to publish your stories no longer."

"And a public apology?" asked Javotte.

Mr. Dover looked at Ms. Rosebud and then to Dr. Cason. "I'm afraid we aren't able to do that," he said.

"Why not?" demanded Norman.

"Because they're not liable for any wrongdoing," explained the lawyer. "It was the courts that found you all guilty, morally, yes, the authors and original publishers could have been found liable if you had taken them to court. Although not impossible, it was doubtful you would have been awarded any compensation. The applicant would have to prove (1) use of defamatory words relating to the plaintiff, (2) publication to third parties, (3) falsity of facts, (4) culpability, and (5) injury. But this is now all hearsay since those responsible are all dead." She looked up from her notes stony-faced.

"Which means?" asked Goldie.

"You're shit out of luck if you think the Babbit's will offer an apology," said Wolfe.

"Crudely blunt, but correct," agreed Mr. Dover.

"So, let me see if I get this straight. You'll give me compensation and agree not to publish the book ever again in exchange for not sending me any more royalty checks," pressed Mr. Stiltskin.

"Exactly."

"Sounds like you guys are getting off easy!" snapped Wolfe.

A sudden murmur like bees in a hive filled the room as they digested the deal placed in front of them. "I think things are going rather well," whispered Javotte to Tisbe. "With a lump sum and that dreadful story forever shelved, we can finally travel and not go incognito."

"Well, I don't like it!" exclaimed Goldie to Norman. "Between my husband's pension and my royalty checks, I can live without worrying about finances. What the hell am I going to do with a lump sum?"

"Invest it," said Ray, who was eavesdropping.

"In what?"

"Gold!" he laughed. "I obviously won't live forever, as you can see," he grinned stroking his white beard. "Take the money and run; that's my motto!"

"I suppose a lump sum isn't such a bad idea," remarked Norman. A sense of peace suddenly overcame the large man as he thought that his story could no longer be published. Naturally, there were old copies around, but gradually they would be weeded out of the libraries and fade away like a bad memory.

"You're both fools!" harped the elderly woman. "Sure, once upon a time, no pun intended, I would have liked the entire bundle. But now, it seems more prudent to take the royalty checks. That way, we have a constant flow of income."

Norman appeared to flounder and now thought more enthusiastically about her logic. "You do have a point," he nodded in agreement.

"Glad to see you're coming on to our side, Norman," said Mr. Wolfe as he lifted his drink and took a long hard swallow. A drop of brandy dripped from his jaw as he surrendered his glass to Salisbury.

"You have some on your chin," Javotte pointed and handed him a cocktail napkin.

"It would be easier if I used a straw," he laughed and nodded appreciatively at the woman. "Funny old spinster," he thought and tossed the napkin on the end table.

The afternoon had created a melodrama in contrast to the invitation's rhetoric of a leisurely few days. Ms. Rosebud looked dubiously at the ring of guests while at the same time, she smiled with quiet satisfaction.

# CHAPTER 5

IT had become quite evident that what was supposed to be a united front had turned into a war of sides. Those who opposed the deliberate split from the publisher slowly made their way around the cribbage board, while those decidedly wishing to maintain the status quo were relegated to the chairs and sofa by the fireplace. Only the hostess, lawyer, and agent remained in their original seats. "Well, that went well," remarked Peri Cason with a helping of sarcasm.

Ms. Rosebud sulked and leaned her chin on her hands. She clutched the cane's pearly handle and exhaled a deep sigh of consternation. "Cheer up!" remarked Mr. Dover, "I've been in negotiations like these before. All I need to do is get in touch with Babbit's counsel and sweeten the pie." He looked at his watch. "It's still relatively early, may I use your telephone?" The eager man rose as he looked to the hostess who pointed in the direction of the open door.

"Use the one in my study," she said.

"Ladies," he replied and turned away.

"Wonder what that weasel is up too?" griped Goldie. Norman turned towards the doorway just in time to see the Dover exit into another room and shrugged. The hostess was feeling betrayed by her guests and brooded. According to her casual interpretation, it was apparent that she had better do something to set the mood right. There was way too much-disgruntled mumbling.

"I must agree with you, Mr. Stiltskin," whispered Javotte, who had found herself sitting between Ray and Tisbe. "I could never have imagined that we would be of the same mind."

"Speak up, sister!" cranked the little man. "I can't hear you."

"She said she agrees with you," parroted Tisbe in a louder voice.

"About what?"

"For heaven's sake, Man, are you daft?"

"Daft? No, I'm not daft, but maybe just a bit deaf," he chuckled.

"We're just surprised that the three of us prefer a payout," clarified Javotte.

"I'm not," Mr. Stiltskin claimed. "You're just as greedy as I am, only you got manners, and I got a big mouth!"

The unlikely trio was now in a heated discussion, while those on the opposing side of the room appeared to ruminate in their private thoughts with Norman bantering back and forth with indecision. "I have such a headache," complained Ms. Rosebud to her lawyer friend. "I did hope my years of research would have amounted to something positive. Now it looks as though I have created a mess."

"The phones are out," Mr. Dover said, returning with a disappointed expression. He sat down and drummed his fingers on his knee as if in serious thought.

"The storm," replied Dr. Cason smiling smugly.

"So it seems," retorted the annoyed man.

"Looks like you'll need to make a decision on your own," Dr. Cason reminded him. But he didn't need reminding; he was already making a mental list.

Ms. Rosebud had moved on from the present matter at hand and began to contemplate dinner when Salisbury glided in looking paler than usual. "It appears we have a problem, Madame," he announced.

"Problem?"

"Yes, Madame."

"And what is this problem?" she asked with impatience.

"It appears that Mr. Jay may be dead, Ma'am."

"Dead?" squealed Roy. "Who's dead!"

"The old sailor," replied Salisbury. A loud gasp of horror suddenly circulated the room.

"Oh, that lovely old fellow," whimpered Javotte.

"Dead, dead, how?" mumbled the hostess, her hands trembling as she tried to lift herself out of her chair but too shaken, fell back into her seat.

"I really couldn't say, Madame. All I can tell you is that when I went in to check on him, he appeared more than asleep. Should I call for the doctor?"

"The phones are out," muttered the hostess.

"Let me check on him," Cason said to Ms. Rosebud.

"I had better go up with you," but as much as she wished, she was too upset to move.

"No, stay where you are, I'll be right back. Salisbury," the lawyer paused, turning to the houseman.

"Yes, I know, I'm coming."

\* \* \*

The bulk of the conversation lay heavy on each member of the party; Mr. Jay had been an innocent victim of a very unlikely circumstance, and the idea that he was lying upstairs dead ignited insecurity over the platter of food served. Questions of "did you eat the strawberries?" passed from person to person, as well as "who ate what?" and "how much was consumed?" There was quite a bit of anxiety growing until Dr. Cason returned downstairs with the houseman trailing behind. "He's not dead," she announced.

"Not dead?" asked Ms. Rosebud, becoming consciously relieved.

"No, but rather weak. I think he needs medical attention as soon as possible." Dr. Cason pulled a bottle of brandy off the davenport and poured herself a healthy glassful.

"Sorry, Madame. My mistake," acknowledged the butler.

"Hell of a mistake, Salisbury!" cried Stiltskin. But as soon as he took a breath, Goldie elbowed him to be quiet.

"Well, that certainly is good news, don't you think so?" remarked Wolfe, pleased that he was more of a carnivore than a vegan.

"Yes, except for the fact that the phones are out, and we can't get help since the roads are flooded," complained Dover.

"Well, there's no need to fret, Mr. Jay is most likely out of the woods. He's sleeping soundly, his breathing isn't labored, and right now, there is nothing more we can do for him. I'm going up to lie down," announced Cason.

"I think I'll do the same," bemoaned the hostess with a rather gloomy expression.

"Cheer up, Tamaya," exclaimed Ray. "It could be worse. It could always be worse."

The two sisters twisted round with snarled expression. "Such poor tact, Mr. Stiltskin," cried Tisbe. But the little man only grinned at her words, relishing the fact that he wholly agreed with her as he watched Ms. Rosebud lean over her cane and take most of the burden up the stairs. He waited until he could hear the two doors shut before speaking. "Now that the mistress is gone, I think you're in line for a good stiff drink."

"Are you speaking to me, Sir?" asked the houseman.

"Who else? You've been on your feet since we got here. You could use a little downtime." There was an impish glimmer in the little man's eyes.

"Very kind of you to notice, Sir," replied Salisbury, not breaking from his character as a dutiful houseman.

"Sure, go ahead, for once Ray is right!" exclaimed Goldie. "Pour yourself a drink and go take a rest. We're not going to tell."

The houseman looked from guest to guest, and each one nodded in silent agreement, that is, except Mr. Dover, who acknowledged by handing the butler a glass of brandy. "Well then, if you all will excuse me," said Salisbury, and accepting the offered drink, he glided out of the room and down the stairwell to his room.

The sound of the rain dropped away as the brandy dampened the urge to talk. Goldie stood up from the comfort of the winged-back chair and caught the eye of Mr. Wolfe. He was smoking, something the older woman hadn't seen him do before. He appeared agitated, and with each exhaled breath, there was a long unfamiliar sigh. It sounded more like a whistle than a note of discontentment. She edged over to the window, knowing Wolfe would follow. "I'm not liking the way things are going," he muttered in a hoarse voice. He mashed the cigarette out in the ashtray and then pinched his eyes.

"You look tired, Wolfe. Why don't you go lie down?"

"I can't; got too much on my mind to sleep," he complained. "I don't know why the hell I listened to my wife. I should know better than to go against my instincts. I've got good instincts," he said.

"Indeed," replied the woman. "But we are here, and we need to convince the rest of these idiots to leave things alone. I don't give a damn about old scores and reputation. It's too late for me as far as I'm concerned."

Mr. Wolfe nodded and pulled the drapes apart. He looked outside; the rain had stopped. "I think I'll go for a walk."

"Now?" she asked incredulously.

"Why not, it's not raining."

"Well, at least go upstairs and get a hat," said Goldie in a grandmotherly voice.

He smiled, but not too widely. "If we can just get Norman to see things our way, we may have a chance of convincing the others over to our side." He turned from the window and pondered his point.

"It's Ray we got to worry about. Norman's a piece of cake. He's always been a pushover. Ray, oh, I remember him from way back. A real devil. Good-hearted if you get to know him, but he's a devil." Her voice trailed off as if there was something else on her mind.

Wolfe liked Goldie, but now she was getting on his nerves. Anyone that had been locked up for as many combined years as they had endured knew the ropes. She might be a sweet little old lady, but even old ladies can be conniving. "Hat, yes, I suppose I should put on my hat and an outer coat. I guess I should'av brought a raincoat."

"We'll continue our talk later," the woman suggested. "In the meantime, I think I'll go up and get my needlework." She looked about the room and noticed the only other person was Mr. Dover, and he was engaged in a book he had taken off the library shelf. She tilted her head but couldn't make out the title. "Can you see what he's reading?" she whispered.

Wolfe squinted and then snorted, "*Beauty and the Beast*," he said.

"Figures," said Goldie coldly, "that bitch got all the good press."

"You didn't like the tale?" laughed Mr. Wolfe.

"Not after she made a fortune from the movie rights. Some people get all the luck."

"Luck?" said Mr. Wolfe. "I don't believe in luck. The only thing I can rely on is my cunning. Trust me; she didn't have luck, just a very good agent."

"And the Beast?"

"That part, my dear, was a fairy tale."

\* \* \*

Wolfe navigated his way down the hill, turning around now and again to see if he were being followed. He refused to take things at face value; the weekend invitation in such close quarters was notably confining. He was markedly impatient, and to say that he was superstitious was an understatement. Dead bodies had gotten him into a world of trouble before, and he cursed the situation he found himself in.

A stand of sycamores stood flat against the sky. Wolfe contemplated whether to take a short-cut across their dark path or to continue along the twisting road. For a fading moment, he stood alone until a call in the silence tore a hole big enough for, "Hello, there!" A peal of laughter rose with the sight of Wolfe's startled expression. "Whoo there, old-timer; sorry to frighten you." Sitting on a swollen log was a youth with a pleasant smile and a look of innocence.

"Old-timer, who are you calling old-timer," challenged Wolfe as he sucked in his stomach and straightened his hat brim below his brow.

"You're one of the guests up at the Rosebud estate, aren't you?" said the boy. He picked a long piece of grass and put it in his mouth.

"And if I am, what's it to you?"

"Nothing, except I'm headed that way to see my father. I expect he's still there," explained the young man. "I'm Reggie Jay."

"You're Mr. Jay's son," echoed Wolfe, and regarding the boy with pity realized he had to choose his next words carefully. There's nothing more flammable than a hot-headed kid. "I don't want you to worry, but your father might have a touch of botulism. Or salmonella, yes, it could be salmonella." Reggie met the statement with little concern and continued to gnaw on the blade of grass. "Either of the two can occur when someone eats food that is, well, bad," Wolfe explained. "Your father ate some strawberries, delicious-looking strawberries if you like strawberries, but I'm afraid he is ..." but before he finished his statement, a woeful expression alerted the boy to trouble.

"Is what?" pressed Reggie, now leery of this sinister-looking stranger.

Wolfe shrugged, "In bed." For an instant, he wished he had not gone down this road; he wished he hadn't met up with the boy and wished he could leave this damned island. He could check the ferry for himself and, if need be, pay someone, anyone, to take him back to the mainland. But that was all wishful thinking, and here he was,

Mr. Do Goodie, placating this youth. "You know, you remind me of someone I know," mumbled Wolfe. And with a trifle more empathy, he trudged back up the hill with the boy in tow.

* * *

Wolfe was huffing and puffing when he reached the front door. His mouth was dry from explaining the situation, except the part he left out where everyone believed Jay was dead. But since the keeper wasn't dead, it was irrelevant.

"I'm not so sure I can go in," Reggie stammered.

"What do you mean you're not sure you can go in?" Mr. Wolfe was feeling put out. His feet were tired, and the only reason he returned was to bring the boy to his father.

"On account of I'm not supposed to be out." The boy slowly raised his chin. "You see, I'm not supposed to be here, on account of…"

"On account of what!" growled Wolfe. He released his hand from the knob and pushed the boy against the door.

"On account that I stole some stuff, not very big stuff, just a few items that nobody was using."

"Great!" Wolfe said, and moving between the boy and the door, he turned and let himself in. "Do me a favor kid, see if you can bring a doctor. We'll take care of your old man." Awakened with the prospect of being in the proximity of a felon, he couldn't take any chances with his parole, and with a quick shove, he pushed the approaching boy back and shut the door.

"Who was that?"

"What are you doing, lurking in the shadows?" Wolfe removed his hat and wiped his feet on the mat.

"I'm not lurking, I heard voices outside, that's all," snapped Norman. "I came down for something to eat." He held his hand out and displayed a half-eaten sandwich. "So, who was it?"

"No one, I must have been talking to myself. I do that sometimes; a bad habit I picked up when I was away." He stepped forward and brushed against the large man. "I would think you would get it." His voice was low and sinister.

"Yea," sighed Norman finishing his last bite. "I get it; I get it all too well."

"Where's everybody?" Mr. Wolfe reached into his pocket and pulled out a pack of cigarettes.

"Not sure?"

"As a rule, the hostess should be the one to announce the next bit of our agenda, but seeing as she's not around, what do you say we retire to the library?" Wolfe lit his cigarette and considered his next move. However, he didn't have to think for very long. A shrill howl hurled from the top of the stairs down to the bottom rearranged the current state of affairs.

"Oh my, oh my, he's been murdered!" Goldie wailed. "Ray's been murdered!"

"Murder!" cried Wolfe and instinctively bounded upstairs towards the cry. A spontaneous opening of doors unleashed shouts of "what's going on?"

"Ray, dead?" Javotte cried out. "Are you sure?"

"How perfectly horrible!" moaned Tisbe.

"Of course, I'm sure, but if you don't believe me, go see for yourself!" charged Goldie and pointing to the last open door she shivered. But it was not from fear. She was dressed in only a silk negligee and clasped the low-cut neckline between her fingers.

"Here, dear," motioned Dr. Cason, and snatching a bathrobe out of the bedroom, she slipped it over Goldie's shoulders.

"Don't go over there, Javotte," Tisbe ordered. "Don't even look!"

"It's not what you think," explained the old woman. "I went to his room to see if he needed anything and when he didn't answer, I went in. That's when I found him dead. We were just good friends, that's all."

"Hmmm. Good friends, I bet you were," scoffed Tisbe.

"Ladies, please!" demanded Mr. Dover. "This is no time to squabble," the portly guest added as he involuntarily moved into the hallway. For him, curiosity and gossip were akin to breathing.

"Perhaps we should stop this tirade and attend to the matter at hand," said Ms. Rosebud hobbling from her room. Grabbing hold of her lawyer friend's arm, she led the meddlesome entourage down the hall, stopping short of entering the little man's room. Only Goldie remained behind to dress. The mood was somber, although filled with a bit of eagerness. "Peri, you go in. The rest of us will stay out here," said the hostess

Lying across the bed was Ray Stiltskin wearing checkered pajama bottoms, a white undershirt, and the face of death. His head hung limply over the side of the mattress with a tightly wound cravat around his neck. It didn't take an expert to see that the man had been strangled. Peri Cason was careful not to touch anything as she walked over the bedsheets that must have been thrown off the bed during the alleged attack. However, what appeared to be out of order was the position of the window. It was cold and rainy, too wet a day to open a window, but it was indeed open, wide enough for a person to slip in and out of. The lawyer examined the sill and kneeled over the carpet; it was damp. She ran her hand along several impressions made from something small and circular, a similar size to the feet of chair legs.

"What's going on in there?" pressed Mr. Dover poking his head into the room.

"He's dead alright," Peri said. "To the best of my observation, he's been strangled."

"Strangled!" cried Salisbury, ascending the staircase with reliable conformity. Dressed in a freshly starched uniform and polished shoes, he was the consummate houseman.

"Yes, presumably with a red ascot," remarked the lawyer.

"Red ascot?" asserted Mr. Wolfe. "Are you sure?"

"Quite sure, it's still wound very snug around his neck," explained the woman, irritated by the challenge

Mr. Wolfe swallowed hard with the words weighted deep in his throat. "You look like you've seen a ghost," said Goldie as Wolfe passed her on his way down the hall. "Hope it wasn't those strawberries."

# CHAPTER 6

---

*10 DAYS EARLIER*

THREE carved figureheads hang on the tavern walls like deer heads over mantles. The black-eyed mermaid peering at the drinkers sitting beneath her buxom torso occupies a commanding spot above the bar; perhaps this is why the tavern was named *The Drunken Mermaid*. A devilish looking maiden with a broken off nose and waxy lips perches above the doorframe. And not to be overshadowed, a golden dragon with pearl-colored fangs is hanging between the two windows, just low enough to remind the patrons to duck their heads if they sit on either side of its extravagant neck. An occasional joker places his cap on its fiery head, at which point, everyone finds this amusing, except for Mr. Lee, the resident face-reader. To Mr. Lee, the dragon is more than a decoration; for him, it's a friend.

"Do you see that man over there?" Ms. Rosebud turned to look. "Not now," whispered Dover with a sharp tongue. "He's looking our way."

Ms. Rosebud ignored the warning and smiled warmly at Mr. Lee, who reciprocated with a gentle nod of the head. "Him? Why that's Mr. Lee. He's the harbor soothsayer."

Mr. Dover glanced over and frowned. "What's he got on, a bathrobe?"

"Don't be so provincial, Harold. Your ignorance is staggering. It's a *changshan;* the traditional robe worn by men." She muttered 'bathrobe' under her breath and picked up her wine glass.

"I still can't believe you ordered wine in here. A beer maybe, but wine?" His voice was reproachful once again.

"You know, if I had known you were a snob, I would never have agreed to come in. But seeing as this is the only tavern dockside, I thought you might like to take in the local sights. Next time, we'll take a cab into town."

"Next time?"

She looked at him with curious eyes and then blew him a kiss from across the table. If this kiss was designed as affection or sarcasm, it was immediately detected by Mr. Jay, who was sitting in the shadows just a few tables away. He wiped his mouth on his sleeve and watched. "So," he thought to himself. "Miss Rosebud's got a secret." He leaned over his drink and listened.

"I have made all the arrangements and now just waiting for confirmation. Wolfe and Ms. Hildebrandt have confirmed. The two sisters are not sure, and the rest are maybes."

"Maybes?" Dover looked disappointed.

"No confirmation either way," she said. "But I suspect they'll all take me up on the offer." They sat in silence for a few minutes as they sipped their drinks. "You can stay over if you want."

"No, thanks," explained the reticent man. "I need to get back to the office, and it's a long drive home, especially since I have to come back in a few days." The woman nodded with understanding.

Mr. Jay took out his pocket watch, a gift from his late wife, and flipped it open. It was time he returned to the lighthouse. However, in a clumsy attempt to remain anonymous, his gangly legs and unchartered lap around the table gained the attention of the man and woman at the next table. "Beg yer pardon, Miss Rosebud," the keeper said as he brushed against the back of her chair. And tipping his cap, he grinned like someone who had come upon something he shouldn't have.

"Why Mr. Jay," exclaimed Ms. Rosebud, her voice ruffling as she spoke. "I didn't see you come in."

"That's 'cause I was sitting over there," he explained, pointing behind him. "But don't mind me, Miss," the salty dog replied. "You continue to enjoy yourselves. Nothing like a good drink on a warm afternoon. Wouldn't you agree?" His interest had visibly quickened as he turned to Mr. Dover and grinned. He tipped up and back on his toes and whistled. "Warmer than usual."

"Mr. Lee is here too," Ms. Rosebud said. "I was hoping he'd come over and tell us a fortune."

"Tell you the truth, Miss," whispered Mr. Jay. "He's as much a fortune teller as I am."

She smiled warmly, "But he adds so much color to the place; without him, this would be just another watering hole." She stroked the outside of her glass as if it were a kitten and then took a sip.

"I suppose," shrugged the keeper. "Well, I better be getting on back to the mistress. She turns sour when I'm gone too long."

"You're married then?" Mr. Dover asked.

"No, didn't say she was my wife, she's my Mother. Now there's a tough bird you don't want to cross. The real lighthouse keeper, she is. I only help." The stout man nodded as if he were interested, but he wasn't and was ready for Mr. Jay to take his leave. But Jay folded his arms to his chest and leaned into the wall, towering over the table. "So, since you and Miss Rosebud have some business to talk over, I guess I'll be leaving." He sighed longingly, needling the couple with his offhanded suggestion.

"Business, what business?" bristled Mr. Dover suspiciously, turning his face upward and hissing like an alligator.

"I don't know exactly; just some business between you and Miss Rosebud. I happened to overhear you two talking, nothing special. I hear all kinds of things. Don't mind what I say; some believe I'm just an old fool," he remarked, and placing his hat on the back of his head, began to step away from the table. "If you want, I'll ask Mr. Lee to come on over."

"Oh, don't bother, Mr. Jay, and please, don't pay any attention to my friend. He's overly sensitive," she said with a cheerful disposition. "Please send my regards along to your Mother."

The seaman nodded agreeably, and while maneuvering between the tables began muttering to himself. A few indiscernible words floated back to the table. "Did that old codger just call me a horse's ass?" stammered Mr. Dover. His eyes pierced the back of the keeper's head as he watched the man exit.

"I do believe he said something like that," remarked his companion. "It was rather stupid of you to even engage in conversation. He does provide a useful function around here being as he runs the ferry."

"But he said that he heard us talking!" whispered the agitated man. "He heard things, Tamaya, things between people are private."

"And as he said, some people think he's a fool."

Harold Dover tossed a few bills on the table and pulled out her chair. "Want me to call you a cab," he asked.

"No, don't bother. I think I'll have a bit of fun with Mr. Lee and stick around. Go on back home, and I'll speak with you in a day or so." She gave him a light peck on the cheek and gently nudged him towards the door like a mother hen. A feeling of relief ignited as she watched Dover exit, and then she turned around. "Mr. Lee, do tell my fortune." Ms. Rosebud leaned her cane by the mystic's corner of the bar and handed him a ten-dollar bill. He looked at her outstretched hand and then pushed it away. "No, I insist," replied the woman and placed it on the counter. "Will you?" she asked again.

The face-reader nodded and slipped off the barstool. "We will sit over there," he instructed and pointed to a table next to the window. "Better light." He rolled the bill and placed it behind his ear like a cigarette and walked gracefully over to the table. Mr. Lee was a slight fellow with bronzed arms and hands. One might say he was flamboyant; he preferred the term colorful. The woman followed him without the aid of her cane with remarkable ease.

He raised his eyes and gestured for her to sit down. She almost expected to see a crystal ball in the center of the table and dared not show her amusement. Mystical silence settled around the table as she sat down. Catching the attention of the barkeep, Mr. Lee raised two fingers. In just a matter of moments, a red-haired waitress slinked over with a tray. "Tea, just the way you like it, Mr. Lee," giggled the girl. "Spiked." He didn't answer; he was too busy examining Ms. Rosebud's face. He pulled his chair closer to hers and closed his eyes. He raised his hands, settling them on the crown of her head, followed nimbly along her brow line, pressing gently down the sides of her face, and then stopping, he cupped just her chin. His lids were sealed shut, and only his head cocked to the side. Then he took his fingers and ran them across her chin and back up the side of her head. He opened his eyes and pulled his hands away. The waitress was hiding behind the post when the sage gave her a hard stare sending her running back to the bar.

"Well?" asked Ms. Rosebud.

"I am thinking," said the soothsayer. "One cannot just spout the first thing that comes out of his mouth."

"I suppose not," agreed the client. She lifted the glass of tea and then set it down quickly. She bowed her head over the rim and blew across the liquid. "Hot," she replied. He nodded, but as if in direct contrast to what she said, he lifted his glass to his lips and slurped greedily.

"I can feel something right here," he said and ran his index finger over her brow. "You are waiting for something," he asserted.

"Yes, I am," she said and wrinkled her forehead.

"This wait, it's been a long time."

"Why, yes, how did you know!"

He looked at her with displeasure, "But there is something or someone who will try to impede what you are waiting for." He reached forward and closed his eyes as he ran his fingers over her cheekbone. "The apples do not lie." He hesitated again, and then with his hands holding her face, he opened his eyes and sighed. "You will have to be patient. It may not be the right time to get what you want."

"You said apples."

"Yes, those are the apples, and yours are not pink but instead sallow." He pointed to her cheeks.

"Well, what can I do?"

He shrugged and then with gusto, drank the rest of his tea. "It is not for me to give advice, only for me tell you to wait."

* * *

When Ms. Rosebud returned home, she felt positively energized. It had taken years to amass her personal library's collection, and after a considerable amount of money, she had finally located the survivors of her classic favorites. Most all the characters had passed on, but the few remaining would be honored guests. She was happy. Nearly all of her career was committed to this project; she cared little for being a librarian, but it was a means to an end. "Where would you like your tea, Madame." It was Salisbury, her favorite houseman. There had been others, but Salisbury was the only one that seemed to understand her needs. Such as now. He was standing before her with the silver tea service.

"Set it in the library, Salisbury. And why don't you join me in a night-cap." Salisbury might be her butler, but he was also a good confidant.

"If you wish, Madame." The man hoped his displeasure was not evident as he followed her and placed the teapot on the table beside the davenport.

"I'll take a sherry and pour yourself what you like. I believe there is still a bit of raspberry brandy in the cabinet."

The observant eyes of Ms. Rosebud noted the animated expression of the houseman as he quoted aloud, "Raspberry brandy, my favorite."

She fingered several books on the shelf and then turned back and sat down empty-handed. "Salisbury, do you find me peculiar?"

"Peculiar, Madame?" Such a question could lead him into trouble. He knew he had to be quite careful with his answer.

"Yes, peculiar, odd, you know."

"I never noticed anything odd or peculiar, Madame."

"You're not just saying that because you're under my employment, are you, Salisbury? Because if you thought so, I do hope you would be honest. I would never hold your opinions against you."

"Naturally, Madame," he lied and took a sip of his brandy.

"Well, I just have the feeling most people find me odd. Well, maybe odd isn't exactly what I mean. No, not odd; maybe eccentric."

"Eccentric?" the houseman said, adding a touch of doubt at the end of the word. "I never thought of you as eccentric."

She was getting irritated now and wondered why she had even brought up the suggestion. "Such uncertainty about one's self can be so unsettling," she thought. Suddenly she wished she was alone. "If anyone was odd, it was Salisbury. The way he slinks around like an oversized cat," she scoffed to herself. "No, he was peculiar, not she!"

The old clock on the mantle chimed nine times. A most reliable clock with its ornate gold hands and white Roman numerals. "I must take my leave, Madame," said the houseman. "Early to bed, early to rise, as the saying goes." He stood up and leaned forward, waiting for her to hand him her glass. "Shall I pour your tea now?"

"No, I'll have it in a few minutes," she contended.

"Is there anything else, Madame?"

A moment slipped away before she spoke. "Then if I am not odd, nor peculiar or eccentric, what then would you say?" she asked.

Salisbury, who hadn't time to come up with an answer, commenced to waver. "Well, Madame, I have never contemplated such a question."

"Nonsense man, everyone has an opinion. I, for one, have my own opinion of you. I think you're a bit of a bore."

"A bore, Madame?" His eyes widened as he kept his composure.

"Yes, a regular stuffed-shirt."

"Thank you, Madame."

"Now, what about me?" she petitioned.

"Well, if I must," he said.

"You must," she demanded.

"You, Madame, are a prig."

"Prig!" she exclaimed, covering her hand over her mouth.

"Yes, Madame, a prig."

"Oh," she said, conceding to his remark. "But not odd or peculiar."

"Absolutely not," he reiterated.

"Well then, that's refreshing. I come from a long line of prigs, you know," she added with contentment.

"Indeed, Madame," agreed the relieved man. "I have met many prigs in my line of work; however, I find you most enjoyable to work for."

"Thank you, Salisbury. I will remember that."

If either party was thinking about the other's opinions, it did not show outwardly. As Ms. Rosebud picked up her book to read, and Salisbury coasted away with unruffled certainty, there was no trace of animosity. Evidently, they had a very satisfying relationship.

# CHAPTER 7

MR. Jay sank into the wingback chair, and although he appeared tired and logy, his appearance was no longer of anyone's primary concern. The dead man upstairs was robbing him of any leftover sympathy. "I never had any trouble eating strawberries before," he attested. "Like I said, never been sick a day in my life from strawberries."

"Well, something didn't agree with you," Norman said with indifference.

"I suppose, but it sure wasn't those strawberries," the sea crab muttered.

"Well, this entire situation certainly is a problem, a huge problem," cried Tisbe aloud. "I would like to abandon this entire adventure and go home.

"I'll second that," grumbled Wolfe.

"I'm afraid you can't until we fix the engine. No one gets on or off this island until then," remarked Jay.

"Well, I am sure there are other vessels we can hire," said Mr. Dover.

"Not really, sonny. This isn't tourist season. Most of the visitors moored their boats, and any skiff out there would be too small to handle the swells."

"What about the police?" announced the agent with callous assumption, "don't we have to get them here to remove Mr. Stiltskin?" A horrified Tisbe shaken by the idea of a corpse recoiled from Dover's insensitive remark.

"Right now, you better just sit tight." Mr. Jay had become emboldened with the prospect that, by proxy, he was the only person who could help this group. And until the weather subsided, no one would be going anywhere without him.

Tisbe sulked with gloomy disappointment. "Cheer up, missy," said Goldie. "If you're lucky, I'll play a little poker with you and whoever else wants to lose their pocket change."

"Aren't you a bit giddy for someone who was in the presence of a dead man just a few hours ago?" charged the sister.

"Well, if I know Ray, and I did, he wouldn't want us all sitting around moping. I believe this calls for drinks!"

"What you are implying is that we hold a wake," said Tisbe.

"Yeah, a wake, or something like that." But the mood in the room was more than grim. Only Mr. Wolfe found the suggestion a good one, after which he took it upon himself to uncork the whiskey bottle. Judging by the half-empty bottle, he wondered if Goldie had already swiped a nip.

"Any takers?" he asked as he poured a shot for himself.

"If it's for Ray, we should all be in," said Norman, and looking around the room, he counted a solemn full house. Everyone was present except Javotte.

"Has anyone seen my sister?" Tisbe asked, looking at her watch. She sipped her drink and glanced up in the direction of the staircase.

"Javotte," she shouted, lifting her voice. "Come on down; we're having a wake."

"Wake hell, you'll wake the dead with that voice!" exclaimed Mr. Dover.

Everyone laughed except Tisbe, who decided to pour herself another shot. "Perhaps I'll go and get her," muttered the sister as she threw the drink to the back of her throat. Reluctantly she set her empty glass on the table and followed the winding banister upward.

The hostess was in deep despair. Her wonderful celebration ruined, as was her reputation. "Just think of it," she whispered to Peri, "in just a few short hours, things have gone from bad to worse. Imagine, a dead man upstairs in one of my bedrooms, and the murderer is sitting in this room."

"Not unless it's Javotte," smiled Peri.

"True, that is true. But I sincerely doubt that prudish woman is the killer."

"And why not," exclaimed Goldie, eavesdropping.

"Simply because she isn't the type."

"Not the type, so what is the type?" Goldie asked.

"Well, someone that is not her, that's all," rebuked Ms. Rosebud.

"You sound pretty sure of yourself," mocked the old woman. "If I were a betting woman, and I am, I'd say you already got your own opinion of who it is."

"Don't be ridiculous!" argued Tamaya. "I haven't the faintest notion of who the murderer might be. Why it could be an imposter, someone who snuck into the house when we weren't looking!"

"An intruder," corrected Peri. "Maybe, maybe an intruder."

"Intruder?" Mr. Wolfe's ears perked up. "I didn't mention it before, but maybe I should have."

"Mention what, Wolfe?" Peri inquired. For a reason she couldn't pinpoint, she felt uncomfortable around this fellow.

"Well, during my walk earlier today, I was met by a young man who claimed he was Jay's son, Reggie, I think he said his name was."

"Reggie!" exclaimed the hostess. "Reggie was here?"

"No, well, yes and no. I sent the boy on his way to see if he could find a doctor for his father."

"Why didn't you mention it before?" Peri asked, asserting a directness usually reserved for the trial box.

"Because it didn't seem very important." He glared defiantly and then continued. "So, if you're looking for an intruder, maybe you ought to start with him." Wolfe sulked back to his chair next to the window and proceeded to look outside.

"It might have been Reggie; I never liked him, not one bit!" scolded Tamaya.

"But what would be his reason. Certainly, the boy had no malice towards Ray. I am sure they had never even met," assured Peri.

The logic was there, but the hostess was not convinced. "The more I think about it, the more I bet that hoodlum had something to do with poor Ray's demise."

"It does seem rather unlikely," added Mr. Dover, who was sitting in his seat like an overstuffed hen on a nest. "There just isn't a motive."

"That we know of," she reminded the two optimists. "Oh, he's a very sneaky boy, came right into this house one time when I was not at home. Had not been for Salisbury, heaven only knows what he might have stolen."

"Did he take anything?" Mr. Dover asked.

Ms. Rosebud sat in judgment of the intruder before executing her response. "No, nothing that I can account for. But the mere fact that he had entered the house through an open window makes him a common criminal in my book."

"Sounds like a boy's prank," Dover said. "Right of passage and all that stuff."

"Dreadful, that's what I say. Dreadful."

"But to accuse him of murder?" Peri asked. "Perhaps that is a bit farfetched. Right now, all our imaginations are working overtime."

"Well, if it isn't that thug, who do you suppose it could be?" There was no mistaking her distrust of each guest as her eyes roamed the room with suspicion.

Mr. Dover slid to the edge of his seat and leaned forward. "Wolfe. If there were anyone to suspect, it would be him." The accuser sank back into his chair and winked at Peri. But apparently, she did not agree with his challenge and nodded a silent "no." "Who then?" he asked.

For the second time this day, she was cornered into offering her opinion but hesitant to provide one. Frankly, she hadn't any. As far as she could tell, it could be anyone in the room. "I'm not sure," she remarked. "We have to weigh all the suspects, and then perhaps one will bubble to the top."

"Well, I recommend no one leaves this room until the authorities arrive," said Dover. "Perhaps you should make the suggestion," he said, turning to Tamaya.

"Me, why me?" she fretted.

"Because you invited everyone here!" exclaimed Dover. "It was your big idea!"

"Don't forget, you had a hand in this too!" she raged.

"Come, come, why all the arguing? It won't help anyone if you lose your heads!" Peri reminded them.

"Yeah!" cried Goldie from the far side of the room. "You're loud enough to wake the dead!" But while her words were intended to break the tension, they didn't, and all she received was an icy stare from Ms. Rosebud.

"Maybe we should play a game," suggested Norman. "It might help us all get out of our foul moods."

"Like what, Russian Roulette?" snubbed Wolfe. The response struck a nervous chord with the guests, all except Harold Dover.

"Well done!" provoked the man as he commenced to clap. "Don't you think Mr. Wolfe is deserving of a round of applause?" He rose to his feet while the hostess sat in panic-stricken astonishment, yet no one else seemed to think this line of talk worthy of a reaction, not even the sharp-tongued Goldie.

"I certainly hope this is not contagious," said Peri.

"What?" asked Tamaya

"This nervous chatter. I've seen it before in other cases. Eventually, someone always cracks, and it's not always a good thing."

"Well, just how long do we have to sit here?" asked Norman, pacing the floor.

"Until the roads are clear," remarked Jay perking up from his chair-nap.

"Crap, and when will that be?" Norman asked, casting blame at the seaman.

There was a long sigh of disgust crushing the spirit of the entire body of guests. The rain tumbled against the windowpane like beads in a bamboo stick. It was a gentle sound, and if it weren't for the undercurrent of the day's insidious event, it would be soothing. But solitude was short-lived, and was suddenly exchanged for a fretful cry of, "He's gone!"

Javotte and Tisbe flew downstairs like a pair of frightened chipmunks, one behind the other. It was almost comical had it not been their sincerity. "It's Stiltskin, he's not there!" cried Tisbe breathless.

"Gone, like he got up and walked away?" said Goldie.

"Ridiculous," remarked Harold.

"It's true; he's not there!" squealed Javotte. "The bed is empty! Go up if you don't believe us." Her hands were shaking, nervously twisting a red piece of cloth.

"My word, what have you got in your hands?" The lawyer eyed the cloth. "Is that what I think it is?"

Javotte looked down, and then as if she were going to say something, the cloth was snatched away. "It was on the floor," she remarked. But Peri's accusatory look startled the woman. "For heaven's sake, what do you think? That I had something to do with that little man's murder?"

Peri unfolded the cloth and then looked from person to person. There was a ring of curious onlookers. "Let me see that thing!" grumbled Wolfe and pulling it free from Peri's hand he held it up and laughed.

"What's so funny?" Harold snapped.

"Nothing," announced Mr. Wolfe and, with a silent sigh of relief, tossed the sash back to the lawyer.

"Where on the floor was this?" Peri asked.

"By the bathroom, the hall bathroom," Tisbe remarked. "But who cares about this when Ray is missing. He can't be dead; I mean dead men just don't walk away!"

"She's right," snapped Goldie, "where the hell could he be?"

"In the wine cellar," said Ms. Rosebud. "I had Salisbury carry him down."

Mr. Wolfe raised his eyebrow. "So, he's in cold storage," he interjected.

"Well, if you want to be crass, I suppose we could say that," Tamaya noted. "We certainly couldn't keep him upstairs for very much longer."

"It wasn't wise to move him," cautioned Peri. "This is a murder investigation."

"Well, I am afraid the police will just have to make do with him elsewhere." Tamaya pulled her cane towards her knees and raised herself. "Why don't you say what's on your mind, Peri. Tell us, who do you think the killer is? If we know, then we can at least get some rest." Her sarcasm was biting, but she was too tired to care. She snatched the red sash and then waved it like ribbons on a kite string. "Does anyone want to claim this?"

But it had now become evident that her announcement intended for theatrics was being tested. The dress Goldie had changed into was a ruby red shirtwaist neatly pressed but devoid of its sash. "It's mine," the older woman said. "I must have dropped it."

Tisbe permitted herself to smile as she made clear of her intentions. "Then it's you!" she charged. "You killed Ray!"

"Don't be an ass!" mocked Wolfe. "All she said was that the sash belonged to her dress."

"Well, if she didn't do it, then who?" sulked the other sister.

The ball was in everyone's court, and the general anxiety of murder had turned into a parlor game. Only Peri Cason seemed to understand the gravity of their situation. She turned her gaze towards the hostess and then along the line of guests. Any one of them could be the killer. "That, my friends, is the mystery," she concluded.

# CHAPTER 8

*The second night*

"I believe you will be among your favorites," said Salisbury. "A most fitting resting place." The houseman lay the corpse on top of a plaid blanket. He didn't know why, but it just seemed in poor taste to leave him on the bare floor. "The Italians are over there," he said, pointing to the rack on the left. "And the French over here," this time pointing to the right. "Unless you want a Chablis, they are in the back." Mr. Stiltskin was beginning to show the physical ravages of his situation, being dead. "You are quite pale now, Sir," said Salisbury. "I will leave you." If this had been his first bout with a body, he might not have been quite so callus. However, a houseman's duties go beyond personal valet or server. He was a man of many trades, and most important, he was an excellent confidant.

\* \* \*

"Mr. Stiltskin is resting comfortably, Madame."

"Thank you, Salisbury. Now, if you could get the weather to clear up, we might have a chance of getting to the bottom of this. Did you turn the air up?" she asked.

"Just a trifle, you know that the reds don't like it much below 55 degrees." She nodded her head and smiled. "Yes, he'll be fine there," she agreed.

"Did he like wine?" the butler asked.

"I imagine Ray was fond of most anything that came in a bottle," she remarked. "He was, however, more of a spirits man."

"Indeed," said Salisbury with regret.

"But we couldn't keep him here by the liquor cabinet, now could we?"

"No, Madame," agreed the houseman. "It would have been most improper." His pause was interrupted by a need to yawn. "Is there anything else I can get for you?"

"One thing, before you retire. Do you think dinner was awkward? I didn't see anyone going back for seconds. Except for Norman."

"I don't think so. Everything was in order, and if I must say so, quite delicious."

"Hmmm, perhaps it was when I sent you to the cellar for more cognac, there seemed to be a lull in the conversation until you returned."

"I hadn't noticed, Madame."

"No, I don't suppose you would have. But I'm very sensitive to these things." She placed her knitting into the bag and then began to speak as if she had retrieved her thoughts. "Just how was Mr. Stiltskin?"

"I believe quite the same as I had left him earlier," Salisbury replied.

"Good," she muttered. "Well, why don't you go on down to bed. I can shut the lights when I go up."

"As you wish, Madame."

Tamaya Rosebud watched as Salisbury glided across the floor and opened the hall door leading to his quarters. His feet never touched the ground, or at least that's what it seemed since she did not hear even the slightest tap of his feet as he walked down the back stairwell. She heaved a great sigh and, with her foot, kicked the knitting basket beneath the ottoman. She was working on a shawl and was almost out of red yarn. "Red," she thought to herself. "It was a popular color today." All that stirred was her breathing and the old clock on the mantle. It had a life of its own and made itself known each hour. She glanced at the gold hands and wondered where the time had been. She was sure the roads would be clear enough tomorrow to send for help.

"It is an unpleasant thing to say, but you are a most cunning hostess." It was a woman's voice, Tisbe's, to be exact. The matron was dressed in a hat and coat and was carrying a small valise. "I'm going to go home, even if my sister doesn't want to."

"At this hour?" questioned Tamaya. "With the phone out of service, I can't even call you a cab."

"Yes, I forgot," and becoming suddenly forlorn, she fell into the chair and began to cry.

"Now, now, I hope you're not weeping on account of Mr. Stiltskin because he is quite all right. Well, as all right as a dead man can be," explained the hostess. "Besides, you can't possibly leave now."

"And why not?" mumbled the upset guest.

"Because you might be the murderer!" expounded Tamaya. At which point, hearing these words, the sister retreated into herself with a series of wails and sobs. "Come, come; I don't really believe you're that upset. You forget that I know you as well as you know yourself!"

"You do?" replied the sister, suddenly appearing to have recovered from her melancholy.

"Certainly, I have every book you and your sister are in. In fact, I have the most comprehensive collection. I am an authority on all of you."

"I imagine they are worth quite a bit of money if they are as valuable as you say."

"Oh, indeed. A small fortune."

This testimony served Tisbe with reason to be more cooperative. "I am afraid that I have been more than rude, Ms. Rosebud. I wish to apologize."

"Thank you, Tisbe, your apology is accepted. Now, what do you say we get to the bottom of all this suspicion? I have an idea that might draw the real culprit out into the open."

Tisbe had, at this time, taken off her hat and coat and was sitting beside a pot of tea. She touched the side. It was still warm. "May I?" she asked.

"Certainly," replied the hostess and offered her a cup.

The two women sat and sipped their teas, and as Tisbe waited, she pondered what Tamaya could possibly have in mind. Finally, she broke the ice. "So, what is this idea you have, I am fascinated to hear."

Tamaya set her cup down and slunk forward in her chair. "Well, have you ever been to a séance?"

"Séance, like one of those occult things?"

"Well, not occult, but spiritual. If we could summon Mr. Stiltskin back, he would be able to tell us who killed him."

"You wish to bring a dead man back to life?" Tisbe tried to sound objective.

"No, not him back from the dead, just his spirit. It's probably wandering around here right now," she said and smiled.

"In this room?"

"Ah, huh. And more likely than not, listening to every word we are saying." Ms. Rosebud could tell that the sister was trying very hard not to appear strained, although she was now unusually pale. "Perhaps we both ought to retire," she suggested and pulled herself up by the arms of the chair. "Tomorrow we will have a séance."

"Tomorrow then," repeated Tisbe and patiently waited as the hostess began to walk from lamp to lamp, shutting off the lights.

"I think you had better get on ahead, Miss Tisbe," she emphasized with her hand hovering over the last lamp. "I wouldn't want you to run into Mr. Stiltskin on your way up to your room." And as she turned towards the light, the frightened woman's silhouette moved quickly up the stairs half-hidden in the darkness of the hour.

* * *

Chairs, one for each of the guests and the hostess, were assembled around the kitchen table cloaked in linen that brushed against the floor, and although it was a tight fit, their placements were well suited for the occasion. The weather continued to be gloomy; however, Mr. Jay insisted that he was well enough to bicycle back to the lighthouse. And although Peri Cason cautioned him that it was unwise to leave the scene of the crime, his conviction as a sailor was greater than her reason for him to stay.

Ms. Rosebud told Salisbury to shutter the windows. "It must be dark, except for candlelight," she explained. "Otherwise, Mr. Stiltkin's spirit might not join us."

"Don't we need a medium?" asked Goldie.

"We are going to summon him with the Ouija board," said Ms. Rosebud. "Now, is everyone comfortable?"

"No, I think Mr. Wolfe's foot is in my space," complained Javotte.

"Your space, your big canoe of a foot is encroaching into my space," snapped Wolfe.

"Please, will you two stop arguing?" nudged Tisbe elbowing her sister.

An anxious ring fell over the room, and it took several minutes for the group to settle down. Norman was making ghoulish faces at Goldie, while Mr. Dover, who was generally composed, pretended his arms were levitating and unable to control their erratic behavior. Even Peri Cason had a difficult time trying not to snicker. Only when Salisbury brought to the table the irregular shaped board and pulled over a chair between Mr. Wolfe and Javotte did the party become serious.

"What about the lights?" Ms. Rosebud asked, turning to the houseman.

"Oh yes, lights," he said. And with a bit of wriggling and pulling out of chairs, he stood up, struck a match to several wicks before shutting off the overhead fixture. This time the tenor of the room had taken on a strangely ominous mood. Ms. Rosebud reached forward and pushed to the center of the table, the Ouija board. Uneasiness in their eyes deepened with the wondering of its painted letters, numbers, and golden drawings of the sun, moon, stars, and other odd symbols. She then placed on it a small heart-shaped plank with three hind legs and a pointer front. "At the right time," she whispered, "Goldie and I will lightly place our fingertips on this planchette."

"The what?" asked Mr. Dover.

"Planchette," repeated Goldie. She glared at the man with disgust.

"When we ask a question," said Ms. Rosebud softly, "the Ouija board will answer by spelling out words and transmit a message from the spirit." Her explanation seemed cryptic yet entertaining for such a dreary day. "But, before we begin, I need everyone to place their hands on the table, close your eyes, and be silent." She waited a moment before administering the next set of instructions. "Now, take hold of the persons' hands seated next to you and be still. Don't peek, Norman!" she scolded. "If you open your eyes, you'll ruin the experience." Convinced that everyone was now in sync, Tamaya held Mr. Dover and Peri's hands and shut her eyes. Masked in stillness, they remained quiet for several minutes until Ms. Rosebud spoke abruptly. "There is an unbeliever among us," she said. "I can feel someone is fighting us."

"Only one," smirked Wolfe. He opened his eyes and scoffed.

"For crying out loud, Wolfe! For once, can you simply go with the flow!" complained Goldie.

"Shhhh," whispered Ms. Rosebud. "The unbeliever is not seated at the table; I believe it is someone else. Yes, it is Clarence, the spirit of the last owner of the house. I have encountered his presence before." Mr. Wolfe opened one eye and peeked. No one else was looking. The entire group seemed as if they were genuinely buying into the idea of a spirit. He felt Goldie squeeze more tightly, a signal perhaps. He closed his eyes and listened.

They remained in this position for several minutes when finally, Ms. Rosebud spoke. "Open your eyes." As if in a hypnotic trance, she signaled for Goldie to place her fingertips on the planchette with hers. "Clarence, are you here?" The words came from Tamaya's mouth but did not resemble her usual speaking voice. No one stirred except Salisbury, who wanted to itch his nose but refrained from moving his hands away from the Javotte's hold. Suddenly the planchette moved effortlessly across the board and spelled out, Y-E-S.

"Can you find Mr. Stiltskin's spirit and bring him here?" asked Ms. Rosebud, in a whisper that ran around the room. The women placed their fingertips on the planchette when something like an impulse whisked the plank across the board.

"I-Will-Try," it spelled.

Mr. Dover, who would have admitted to being a skeptic, appeared astounded. "It's talking to us!" he uttered loud enough for all to hear.

"Shhhhh," chastised Salisbury.

The room was tomblike as all parties remained deathly silent. "Clarence, are you still here?" asked the voice that now resembled an Italian waiter.

Suddenly the planchette shot across the board and pointed to the letters Y-E-S. Goldie's heart thumped with anticipation.

"Is Ray with you?" the possessed asked. All eyes were on the planchette. Goldie's fingertips were barely touching the plank when the question was posed again, only this time with the pageant of combat. "IS RAY WITH YOU?"

The planchette that had once led to definitive responses began to make circular motions; slowly at first and then gathering momentum, it darted from corner to corner. "What's going on?" asked Peri. But as the medium continued to demand Ray, neither woman's fingers could remain planted on the erratically moving planchette. "No, Clarence, no!" the voice shouted just at the moment the plank soared in the air.

"The candles," someone shouted. "They've gone out!"

"What's happening?" cried Tamaya. Pandemonium and darkness enveloped the room.

"Open the shutters!" demanded Peri as she reached for what she thought was the window.

"That's my head," grumbled Mr. Wolfe. "Everyone stop!" he called out. "I've got a match!" But no sooner did he strike one, did Salisbury throw open the kitchen door emitting light to shine on a most ill-fated scene.

"Good lord, I think you killed Javotte," bellowed Norman.

"Javotte?" squealed Tisbe.

"You got some tact, Norman," cried Goldie.

"What did I say?" he muttered.

"Oh, good heavens!" Bending over her white cane, Ms. Rosebud scrutinized the prone body of the woman. It was quite evident that the planchette struck the poor woman in the temple when it flew from the table. "Good heavens," she said again.

"Looks like Clarence had it in for Javotte," said Mr. Wolfe to Salisbury.

"Indeed, so it appears, Sir. A most unconventional way to pass." The houseman, noticing the hostess's distressed state, glided over to her side. "Would you like me to take her to see Mr. Stiltskin, Madame?"

"Let's wait for the sister to say goodbye," whispered Tamaya pointing to the floor where Tisbe was kneeling over the motionless woman cradling her head. A trickle of blood was seeping from the temple.

"Very well, Madame. I do believe this is your most lively séance to date."

"Perhaps, but it is rather unfortunate, we were so close to finding out the truth. We've never had a tragedy, have we Salisbury?"

"Not to my recollection," he agreed.

"I don't know about you, but I could use a stiff drink," said Mr. Dover. "Join me, Wolfe?"

Any animosity that the two men felt for each other seemed to have extinguished. "You know, you're not such a bad guy after all," Wolfe declared as he followed Dover into the library. "After a few whiskeys, I just might get to like you."

\* \* \*

The woman's skull had indeed been severely compromised. Ms. Rosebud poked the planchette with her finger and scowled. "It hardly looks lethal," she acknowledged.

"Well, if I had to offer my scientific analysis, which I will, its flight from the table struck at just the right trajectory to administer a severe blow and cause Javotte to collapse, fall off her chair, and hit the floor."

"Two blows in one," remarked Salisbury.

"You might say that. Until an autopsy is performed, however, it is uncertain as to which event caused the fatal blow. Nonetheless, it evidently hit a very vulnerable spot." Peri tapped her temple as if those listening needed reminding.

Ms. Rosebud's demeanor looked curiously composed for a woman who just had a second guest die in her home. "At least it isn't murder," she said with a sigh of relief.

"Not unless she was dead before she hit the floor!" Goldie chimed in. "What if someone hit her, and that thing had nothing to do with it!" she contrived, picking up the planchette.

"Put that down," demanded the lawyer. "We can't tamper with any of the items in question until the authorities arrive."

"So, we should have left the old gal here in the kitchen?" Goldie asked, displaying her disapproval for Peri's scolding.

"Heavens, no," replied the hostess. "Salisbury had the decency of placing her with Mr. Stiltskin. We simply couldn't walk around the dead woman all day, now could we?"

"Oh, I bet Ray loves that," howled Goldie. "He had such a fondness for her!"

# CHAPTER 9

"THAT makes two," said Harold.

"Two what?" Norman asked, pacing like a junkyard dog.

"Two dead, what else?" Harold Dover spouted with contempt for the other's ignorance.

"How the hell am I supposed to know what you're talking about." The large man was restless. "If the cops don't get here soon, I'm just leaving."

"And incriminate yourself? It doesn't seem like a smart move for a man who got out on early parole."

These words called for a moment of reflection, which Norman couldn't disagree with. "Well, it seems as though things are moving too slow for my taste."

"Why don't you go for a walk. I'm sure the grounds can't be that waterlogged if Jay got out unscathed."

"We are assuming he's okay," Norman clarified. "Maybe he's lying in a ditch with his head smashed in by the murderer."

"My, what a morose image," laughed Dover.

"Well, it is possible. Anyway, if I don't get out of this house, I might go crazy. I don't like to be penned in."

Harold Dover wasn't a compassionate man; however, he couldn't help but feel sorry for him. "Want me to go with you?" he asked. "I could do with a stretch."

Norman's long mouth curled up at the corners as he lazily walked to the window and pulled aside the curtain. "Looks like a lull in the weather. Sure," he nodded, turning around. "I'll go get my coat and hat and meet you out front."

The smell of wet air entered the foyer as Harold Dover opened the door. The sky was the color of slate, and the distant trees looked more brown than green. The outside world had absorbed the faint odor of mud. He wasn't in the mood to traipse over puddles and soggy leaves, and now wondered why he had suddenly suggested going too. He walked back into the house and waited at the bottom of the stairs. He couldn't see much further than the first doorway at the top of the landing. This was Tisbe's room, and the door was shut. "Hey Norman, what's taking you?" He climbed several steps listening for the big man. "Norman, let's go," he called again. This time the first door opened and the sister shuffled alongside the banister and peered down.

"He's not here," she said. Her voice strained as she spoke.

"Where is he?"

"Out, he's been out since breakfast. Don't you remember, he said he was going for a walk." She folded over the railing, and like a marionette, her head bobbed while she spoke. "It was you who suggested he go."

"At breakfast this morning?"

"Yes, now, if you don't mind, I'm going back to my room." Dover heard the door slam shut. The woman had disappeared.

"At breakfast, no," he decided. The shock of her sister's death must have made her hallucinate. "I was standing in the library just minutes ago when we decided to go for a walk," he recalled. "Damn that old fool and damn this whole weekend."

"That's quite a bit of damning, Harold," remarked a voice. It was Ms. Rosebud, her eyes glowing hotly, and she moved as if in a dream.

"It's that woman up there, Tisbe. She's trying to gaslight me."

"Now, why would she do that?"

Harold slinked back down. The hostess was leaning against the banister, one hand on the rail and the other on her cane. "I don't know, because she's nuts."

"Come and have a cup of coffee with me, Salisbury has put on a fresh pot. We can go into the kitchen and fix it to our likings."

"Are you sure you know how?" he asked snidely.

But Tamaya pretended not to hear and followed the noise of the percolator into the kitchen where arranged on the table were cups, spoons, and a silver sugar tong. "I do prefer sugar cubes, don't you?" the hostess asked as she plucked one from the bowl and dropped it into her cup.

"You forget, I take mine black," grumped the man.

The percolator finally calmed down and was now making an occasional "pop pop." "I didn't forget; I never knew that," she remarked. Dover scowled at her candor. She knew damn well how he took his coffee, but he wasn't about to debate it with her now. "So, where were you going this morning?" she asked.

"Ran into Norman. He was in a bit of a snit, so I convinced him to go with me on a walk, but he slipped away without me."

Tamaya sipped her coffee, it was hot and sweet, just the way she liked it. "Do you suppose he'll come around?"

"Come around?"

"You know, come around and take your deal."

"Heavens, Tamaya, with all that's gone on, I haven't even given it a thought." He looked at her face; the skin was still as smooth as a pearl. He could tell that she wasn't kidding. "I don't know what he'll do. It's ironic; Ray and the sister were all ready to sign." He shook his head and merely laughed with disgust. For a moment, he appealed to his instincts and allowed it to dominate his inner thoughts. Releasing the tension in his jaw, he smiled. "On the other hand, since those two met with such an unfortunate demise, there's more money in the pot to convince the others to take my offer."

"You're forgetting something important, aren't you? One of them is most likely the murderer."

Suddenly the coffee tasted bitter, and he set the cup down on the saucer. "And then again," he complained, "maybe not."

\* \* \*

Mr. Wolfe handed Peri Cason a book of matches from his shirt pocket. "Since when did you take up smoking?" he asked.

"Since you just offered me a cigarette," she laughed. She struck the match and put the flame to the end of the cigarette. She inhaled slowly and then exhaled. A billow of smoke fluttered out of her newly formed smile. "You know," she remarked. "I don't know your first name. Everyone simply calls you Wolfe."

"I like to keep my business to myself," he remarked and tucked the pack of cigarettes back into his pocket.

"Even your name? Don't you think that's a bit close vested?"

"I suppose, but I'm used to being called by my last name. In prison, you lose your identity."

"Well, if you don't mind me asking, what is your name?"

"But I do mind," he retorted and grinned. This time he didn't worry about showing his teeth.

"Suit yourself, but when the police come, they'll want to know."

He motioned in agreement and leaned back into the sofa. "Martin," he said.

"Martin?"

"Yes, my name is Martin."

"Oh, that's a nice name."

"Martin Wolfe, but my wife calls me Marty. She's the only one I allow to call me Marty, and my mother."

"Does your mother live with you?"

He turned and pierced the woman with a peevish frown. "Why would my mother live with me?"

"Oh, I don't know, lots of people live with their mother."

"Do you?"

"No, I guess it was a strange question. My mother has long passed."

"Mine too, except now that I think of it; she does live with us. On the shelf, in an urn…if, you know what I mean."

The lawyer nodded and wondered why she had opened such a strange line of questions. "Mine is in Georgia, but not in an urn."

Mr. Wolfe glanced up at the clock and then back at the woman. Something was unsettling about her, and he began to wonder if she was the murderer. She acted so "high and mighty," questioning everyone with her legalese; her entire persona could be a front. Oh, he knew that kind. Yes, he decided, she may well have designed the perfect con. Lawyer friend indeed, more like a killer! His pupils dilated with the mere thought, and at once, he began to scheme. How could he discreetly warn the others of this imposter?

"Something bothering you, Wolfe?" Peri asked.

Wolfe felt himself flinch. "No," he lied, "just thinking about our situation. It is pretty unnerving to think someone in our party might be a killer. Don't you think?"

"I haven't thought of anything else."

"Then I say, we gather everyone together and make a list. Yes," Wolfe stressed, asserting authority, "a list of motives, maybe we'll flush the truth out that way."

Peri crushed the cigarette out in the ashtray. "You know, Wolfe, I believe you have an excellent idea."

\* \* \*

"You're not even listening to a word I have said," crabbed Goldie. The woman dropped the book on the library table and shoved it towards Wolfe. Then she pulled five others from off the shelf and lined them up side-by-side.

"It doesn't prove a thing," he said.

"Well, it certainly is a slap in the face. To come all this way and not see mine with all the rest is damned insulting!" She peered at him over her eyeglasses.

"Don't do that!" he said.

"Don't do what?"

"That! Don't give me that look. It reminds me of someone."

Goldie smiled and slid her glasses down the bridge of her nose. "Grandma?" she smirked.

"Cut the shit, will you, Goldie!"

"Well, I'm sorry, but I'm miffed. I want to know why there isn't a book about me?"

"Why don't you ask Tamaya instead of getting annoyed with me?" he suggested.

"Ask me what?" Ms. Rosebud entered the library like a cat. She honed her words like a knife, sharp and direct.

"Ask you, why you don't have a book about me?"

"I most certainly do," the hostess insisted. "Yours's one of my favorites." For several quick moments, she perused the shelf, scanning it up and down but retrieved nothing.

"Well, it must have been discarded," goaded Wolfe. He enjoyed sparing with Goldie and hoped to get another rise out of her.

"Maybe one of the guests is reading it?" suggested Tamaya.

"Nonsense, we all know each other's story. No, I think there's something more insidious going on," Goldie proclaimed, having now planted a seed of doubt in the librarian's mind.

"Who would want it?" ribbed Wolfe. "If you ask me, it was a random pick. The person just closed their eyes and took the first book they touched."

"But nobody asked you, Wolfe," scorned Goldie. "Nobody wants your lousy advice. Since when are you an expert on literature?"

"Well, are you?" he asked, trying to even the score.

"Actually, yes. I worked in the library at the women's penitentiary," she gloated.

"You mean you passed out books to your fellow inmates!" he laughed.

"And you, what did you do?"

"Worked in the dispensary," he said.

"Oh, a pill pusher!" Goldie smirked.

"More like a medic," he grinned.

"Please! The two of you are giving me a headache with your arguing!" cried Tamaya and falling back into the armchair, she began to whimper like a child.

"Geez, what got into her?" asked Goldie.

"I haven't the slightest idea?" Wolfe said. "Maybe she needs some alone time. Want to get some coffee?"

"Thought you'd never ask."

The burdens of the day were leaning heavily upon the hostess. She patted her eyes with her handkerchief and brooded. The house was humming with idle chatter that she was unable to discern. She wished Salisbury would come into the library to bring her some tea. However, she quickly forgot her desire for tea at the sight of her dear friend at the doorway. "Come and sit down; I have something to ask you."

Peri Cason was wearing a pair of khaki walking shorts and a starched white blouse. In comparison to the hostess, she suddenly felt self-conscious. "I have decided to dress more casually while I'm here," she remarked in an almost apologetic tone. "Besides, while I'm sleuthing, I need to be flexible in case I have to get on the floor looking for evidence."

"I dare say I hope it doesn't come to crawling on hands and knees," imagined the librarian. She patted the adjacent chair and beckoned for her friend to sit.

"So, what's on your mind besides two dead bodies in your wine cellar," the woman joked. But her words did not get the reaction she expected out of her friend. "You look as though something has spooked you, Tamaya. What's up?"

"Well, it isn't anything that was said, exactly, it's a feeling I have," the woman confessed, leaning in towards her friend. "I must admit that I usually have a good read on people. It's Goldie; I have a feeling, an awful feeling that she might be,"

"The killer?" gasped the lawyer.

"Shhh, not so loud. I don't know. She's got a jealous streak a mile long."

"You just noticed," Peri said with sarcasm. "Why she was almost a tigress when it came to Ray Stiltskin. Heaven helps the other woman that would have gotten between her and that little man."

"No, it's not about Ray; it's her book. You see, the book about her is missing," Tamaya explained.

"What's missing?" scoffed Mr. Dover peering down from behind Ms. Rosebud's chair.

"Good Lord, Harold! You scared me to death. What are you doing sneaking around?" Tamaya scolded and slapped his hand.

"I'm not sneaking, just prowling!" he laughed. "What's missing?" he asked again.

"Didn't your mother teach you not to eavesdrop?" the lawyer asked.

"Eavesdrop? My good woman, I merely stepped into the room and happened to catch a few words. Naturally, I want to know what's missing." He sat down and making himself more than comfortable, put his feet up on the ottoman, and slipped off his shoes.

"It's one of my books, one about Goldie; I think it may be misplaced."

"Misplaced? How can something of such value be misplaced? You suppose it was stolen?" he suggested, glancing from woman to woman.

"I don't know, it could be, but who would want it?" she asked naively. "Certainly, no one here. They aren't interested in these books."

"But maybe the murderer is?" he proposed.

"To tell you the truth, I was in here not too long ago reading to Salisbury. Nothing looked out of place," Tamaya speculated, trying to recall the evening's events in question.

"Well, it doesn't seem like a tough thing to sort out. Just ask Salisbury," Harold snapped impatiently.

"Yes, I could, couldn't I?" Tamaya thought aloud, yet her unnerving feelings about Goldie continued to badger her.

"I'm sure it will turn up," assured Peri Cason. "Right now, we have a bigger problem; the killer could strike again."

"And this time I'm ready!" the pretentious man touted. And bending over, he pulled his trouser leg up and removed a small pistol from a holster strapped to his calf.

"For crying out loud, are you out of your mind!" cried the lawyer.

"On the contrary, my dear, I haven't been more sane in my entire life."

* * *

"It appears that someone is missing," Goldie said as she counted heads. "Where's Norman?"

"Norman went for a walk hours ago," Wolfe replied. "I thought he'd already returned; maybe he's napping?"

The doubt in his voice led Mr. Dover to look at his watch. "I can't imagine the big guy would miss cocktail hour; 6:00 p.m. straight up."

"5:55," corrected Peri Cason, pointing to the clock on the mantle. "You're fast."

"And maybe that old timepiece is slow," Harold chided.

"No, Sir, the Triton has not missed a minute since it's been keeping time," Salisbury said. "I believe it must be your Longine that has skipped ahead. Cheese puff?" Mr. Dover scowled as he shooed the man away. His exaggerated sigh reflected disgust.

Tisbe sat in the oversized armchair and stared into her drink with faraway eyes, deaf to her surroundings. "Do you think Mr. Jay will return?" she asked, looking up from her glass. "Maybe I should call him."

"The phones are still out, Madame. Perhaps a cheese puff will lift your spirits," Salisbury said as he offered the hors d'oeuvres.

"Javotte and I had so many plans," the bereaved whimpered. "Now that we're getting a settlement on our book, we were going to make plans. All she wanted was to make plans."

"Who said anything about taking the deal," cried Goldie. "We never decided on the deal; it was you two and Ray that wanted the whole enchilada at once."

"And now with your sister out of the picture," mused Wolfe, "you'll get the entire settlement all to yourself."

"That's not true!" whelped the sister. "That's cruel, just plain cruel!"

"There's no enchilada to split because there's no deal!" repeated Goldie.

"Not unless Norman wants to make a deal." reminded Wolfe.

Ms. Rosebud, who seemed to have woken up from a catnap, tapped her cane on the floor. "I don't think this is a good time for business negotiations, do you?"

"Apparently, yes," Wolfe said snidely.

"Frankly, I believe we have a more demanding situation to address," the lawyer began. "Like the matter of two murdered guests."

"Murder, who said anything about Javotte being murdered!" exclaimed Tisbe. "It was an accident, a terrible accident. I can't bear to think anyone would have wanted to see her gone!"

But the lack of unanimous agreement to Tisbe's announcement only fertilized the sister's imagination. "Oh, you don't think anyone actually killed her?" she asked. "Who, who would do such a thing?"

"The same person that took out Ray!" snipped Goldie.

"And Mr. Norman," announced Salisbury returning with a full platter of cheese puffs.

"What!" screamed Ms. Rosebud.

"Mr. Norman, Madame," Salisbury said, "it seems that he has met with a most unfortunate accident."

"For heaven's sakes, man, where is he?" demanded Dover, at which point hearing the distressing news, spilled whiskey on his cravat.

"By the trash bins, a most unpleasant place to find oneself dead," claimed the houseman. "It appears that he may have tripped and fallen on the cobblestone."

"Oh no, oh no!" cried Tisbe.

"Are you sure he's dead?" Wolfe asked with skepticism. "The last time you delivered such a claim, Mr. Jay was indeed alive and not, as you stated, dead."

"No, Sir, this time, I am quite certain. Mr. Norman's head, as hard as I imagine it was, is not that resilient."

"Good Lord, Salisbury!" the lawyer gripped. "Could you be any more graphic?"

"I think not, Madame. I am merely giving you my observations."

"Oh, this is more than I can bear!" shrieked Tisbe.

"Shut up, woman!" cried Goldie. "You're making us all nervous with your comments."

"Thank you, Goldie; I couldn't have said it better myself," Harold acknowledged. "Now, if you'll excuse me, I must go up to change before dinner since I smell like a distillery."

"Change, how can you think about changing at a time like this?" the incensed attorney demanded.

"Oh, let him go," interjected Tamaya. "He'll be down in a minute. Besides, we have to take Norman to the cellar."

"Cellar!" disputed Peri.

"Certainly, we can't let him stay outside overnight. No, he must be brought inside like the others."

"Others?" Peri repeated.

"Don't be coy, Peri! She means with Ray and the old gal!" taunted Goldie.

"Do you need help, Salisbury?" the hostess turned her attention to the houseman, who had finally set the cheese puffs on the side table.

"I believe I will manage, Madame. I can use the garden wheelbarrow to transport him."

"Good thinking, Salisbury," she said and smiled meekly.

"Poor Norman, what a way to go. I mean years of climbing trees and stalks, never taking a header, and now, to end up falling off his own clumsy feet." Goldie shook her head with regret.

"Or did he?" Peri asked. "If no one minds, I'm going outside with Salisbury. It is more than likely that we have another murder on our hands."

"Then I'm going too, just in case Salisbury needs some help," Wolfe echoed. However, it was not his benevolent nature that guided him but rather his suspicions concerning the lawyer. As for Peri Cason, she concealed the same misgivings about Mr. Wolfe.

"So, it's just us three ladies," Goldie acknowledged, pushing the platter of cheese puffs in her direction. She popped one in her mouth just as she caught Tisbe turning away. "What?" implored the older woman wiping her greasy fingers on her napkin.

"Nothing," Tisbe lied.

"No, really, what? You were staring at me! What's the matter?"

"No, I wasn't!" Tisbe said.

"Yes, you were," concurred Ms. Rosebud. "I saw you staring."

"See, you're a liar!" squealed Goldie and then grabbing another cheese puff she stuffed the entire pastry into her mouth and slowly chewed while making deliberate exaggerations with her lips.

"It's just that I was thinking; one of us could be the murderer," Tisbe alleged.

"Is that all?" countered the hostess. "I thought it was something else."

"Like what?" Tisbe asked, turning her mouth downward.

"That you were wondering how to kill me!" suggested Goldie with a sinister tone.

The sister sprang up in her chair as if suddenly inflating. "You, why would I want to kill you?"

"To get me out of the way, after all, I am in the way of you getting the deal you want," Goldie charged.

"And I am in the way of you getting the deal that you want!" retorted Tisbe wagging her finger.

"Oh bravo!" quipped Tamaya, delighted by the exchange of accusations. "This is a regular chess match, and it's clear that you're both in check. But with Norman headed to the wine cellar, you have only Mr. Wolfe to contend with!"

"It sounds like you're accusing one of us as being the killer!" growled Goldie.

"Oh, heavens, I was only joining in the fun," taunted the hostess. "How could such sweet old ladies be killers?"

"Easy," said Harold adding to the conversation. His unexpected interruption caused Ms. Rosebud to clasp her hand to her heart.

"There you go again, sneaking around!" cringed Tamaya.

"For your information, I was not sneaking, I was simply walking quietly," Dover explained. He had changed into a well-pressed shrimp colored shirt, black pleated trousers, and smelling of musk-scented aftershave.

"Phew, what's that? Is that you, Dover?" Goldie asked, holding her nose.

"If you mean, am I wearing a new men's cologne, the answer is yes."

"Well, don't sit next to me," she declared. "You smell sort of like the outdoors. Moose-like," she snickered. "Like a big pink moose!"

"I think it's a very nice smell," defended Tisbe. "Very manly."

"Thank you, Tisbe," Harold said and sat down in a chair between the hostess and Tisbe. "Now, I was going to say that there is no reason an elderly woman couldn't be a killer."

"He's right, you know," interrupted Tamaya. "I have many books where the old woman is not as innocent as one would like to imagine. Just the other day, I was reading that book about those two adorable children lured into the cottage of…"

"Spare me the bedtime story," interjected Goldie. "We all know the tale of Hansel and Gretel."

"Case in point," Harold smirked. "So, you must admit, we cannot exclude anyone by proxy of age or gender."

"I do wish Salisbury would return and bring us more cheese puffs," Ms. Rosebud lamented with full intentions of changing the subject. Trading barbs with Harold was more than exhausting. She leaned wearily against the handle and raised herself from the chair. "What could be taking them so long?"

Goldie shrugged her response and then eyed Ms. Rosebud as she propped her cane against the armrest and wandered over to the mantle. She picked up the clock and then set it down.

"Well, I'll be," exclaimed the older woman. "I thought you couldn't walk without your longnecked companion." She reached over and pulled the cane to get a better look. Custom made with a white beechwood shaft, classic derby handle, and pearl collar. "Fancy!" she cooed. "It's even got little rubber tips." Goldie lifted the end for Tisbe to see.

"Oh, I think you'd better get another tip, Dear, this one seems to be discolored," remarked Tisbe pointing out the flaw. But there was something in the tone that prevented Tamaya from finding a polite response. Instead, she turned to look, but in her haste lost her footing.

"Heavens!" exclaimed the spinster. "You're lucky the mantle shelf was there for you to grab!"

Tamaya nodded as Goldie handed the woman back her cane, eyeing her with distrust. "I'm not as sure-footed as I used to be," Tamaya explained. "I often react too quickly, and then, the next thing you know, I'm like a fish out of water."

"Or up the creek without a paddle," mocked Goldie.

"I don't know, I thought you did a great job without that thing the night at the harbor bar," Harold said.

"Harbor bar?" Goldie asked with interest. "You mean to tell me we've been held up in this stuffy house and not too far from here is a tavern?"

"Oh yes," piped in Tisbe. "Right before we arrived, Javotte and I stopped in for a glass of port."

"Port my eye," winked Harold.

"Well it was, you can ask my sist..." but the words suddenly got caught in her throat, and she stopped abruptly. "It was port," she whispered. "Just port."

Goldie turned her nose up at the sister and sat back quite content, resting her feet on the ottoman. She wriggled about for a moment until she found the most comfortable position and sighed like a dog. "I better not get too comfy," she announced, "look who's back!" The old woman grinned, observing the strangely composed entrance of both Wolfe and Peri Cason.

"Well, he's dead all right," admitted Wolfe. "Bloody mess too. Poor guy, whoever killed him must have come up from behind. A man like Norman was too strong to have been taken down unless surprised."

"But don't you think he would have heard someone approaching?" Tisbe asked.

"Not if the person snuck up, he was hard of hearing. Didn't you notice his hearing aid?" Peri looked around the room, but there was not a glimmer of recognition to her statement.

"Hadn't noticed," shrugged Goldie. "All I know is he was a decent guy."

"Which also means one of us must be the killer," fretted Tisbe.

"Or not, maybe it was someone else. Someone who had it in for you!" squealed Goldie pointing at Ms. Rosebud. "Someone that wanted to ruin your reputation as being the worst party-giver EVER!"

Wolfe winked at Goldie and smirked. "Well," he said, "there's only one thing left to do. No one can leave this room until the police arrive."

"No one?" remarked the hostess. "Oh, we must make an exception for Salisbury. If not, we'll all be very sorry if he can't continue to do his duties."

"I agree, Salisbury can leave, but no one else," proclaimed Goldie, who was looking at the empty platter of cheese puffs.

All found this to be acceptable. "Well then, perhaps it is time to get down to serious business. I suggest we go around the room and offer a reason and motive as to who the killer could be. If you all agree, I will take notes," suggested the lawyer.

"That seems fair," Ms. Rosebud said. "Like an old fashion parlor game!"

"And then what?" asked Wolfe ignoring the hostess's insipid remark.

"We'll leave that up to the police," blurted Tisbe.

A strain of discomfort settled around the room as if someone had suddenly released a most unpleasant smell, yet no one admitted that it had the stink of danger.

# CHAPTER 10

---

## Two months earlier

"REGGIE, I thought we brought you up better!" Jay waved the stolen book in front of the boy who, only moments ago, was entertaining a peaceful breakfast.

"Why do you want to go and ruin his eggs?" the grandmother asked, snatching the book away. "Let him eat first and then wallop him!" She scanned the cover before setting it aside. "Looks old, maybe valuable," she remarked, eyeing the boy. Then without warning, she slapped the back of his head.

"Grandma! What'd you do that for?"

"For being a thief!" she said and swatted him with the dishcloth.

Jay picked the book up off the table and began to leaf through. Although the pages were dry and yellowing, the gold letters still shimmered. "I ought to make you return this book yourself and confess that you stole it!" he threatened. "The only reason I won't make you confront Tamaya Rosebud is that we live on this island with her, and it would be too damn humiliating if she knew my boy was a common criminal."

"What are you going to do, Jay?" asked the old woman. She was beginning to assess the book as possessing more than words.

"It needs to go back to where it belongs; it's got to be returned," gripped the father, breaking off in a tenor of disgust.

The old woman eyed her grandson as a cat eyes a mouse. "Are there more of these?"

"Mother!" exclaimed the man.

"I was only asking. I've heard that books like this cost quite a bit of money. I imagine Ms. Rosebud must be at her wit's end searching for it."

Reggie turned towards his grandmother, "Probably doesn't even know its missing," he said.

"Doesn't know?" the woman repeated.

"Most likely not, she's got a whole library full of books like these," he confessed while interpreting her expression. But he couldn't tell what she was thinking since she was wearing her poker face. She was the happiest when she was feeding someone. However, right now, she was not feeling generous towards her grandson and lifted his plate away. He discovered at an early age that his grandmother was a force to be reckoned with, and a voice in his head told him to be still. He inched back in his chair as his father sat down and reached for the coffee set before him.

"Careful, it's hot," she cautioned.

He acknowledged the warning with a wink and slurped. "It's good, Ma." He clutched the mug and, without looking up, spoke. "Take the book back, and don't get caught."

"How?"

"I don't know how but take it back."

"Grandma, tell him I can't."

"What do you mean you can't?" the grandmother challenged. "You figured out how to get it the first time." Then, just for good measure, the old lady slapped the boy on the back of the head.

"Grandma, why'd you do that?"

"To remind you that you'd better listen to your father!" she snapped and handed him the book.

Stealing something seemed much easier than returning it. When he snuck into the house by way of the back window, there was a thrill. But now that he had to get it back inside, the excitement was extinguished. At least he didn't have to take it back right away, neither one of them said when. For an instant, he felt relief as he made his move towards a formal atonement. "Okay, Grandma, okay."

"That's my boy, Reggie! Now, go on up to the lighthouse and get on with your watch." Out of the corner of his eye, he thought he saw his father smile, but he didn't dare turn to look. A truce had been declared, and for now, he was in the clear.

# CHAPTER 11

---

IT was a strange sight when Salisbury returned to the library. It was not the tray of tea sandwiches, but rather the book it was balancing on that was out of place. "I found this when I was straightening up," the houseman said, setting the platter on the table. He handed the book to Ms. Rosebud and straddled the empty tray by his side.

"My book!" exclaimed Goldie.

Tamaya turned it over in her hand and then rested it on her lap. "Where did you find it!"

"In Miss Tisbe's room, Madame. It was on the nightstand." The explanation was immediately embraced, and all eyes fell upon the sister.

"I can explain!" Tisbe cried, dodging silent accusations. "I didn't know it was yours, Ms. Rosebud. It was given to me."

"Given to you?" repeated Peri softy.

"Yes, really, the night Javotte and I first arrived. I told you, we went into the tavern for a glass of port."

"Whiskey!" scolded Goldie.

"Let her talk!" instructed Peri. "Go on, Dear," the lawyer said, turning to the sister.

"We were sitting at a table when a boy, no, a youth, came up and said he had a book that he thought we might like to read. We told him we weren't interested. But then he said it was valuable and had overheard we were going to be visiting Ms. Rosebud. He asked if we would take it there because it belonged to the lady of the house."

"And who was this boy?" Wolfe interrupted. "I don't suppose you remember his name. Or perhaps I might assist you. Was his name Reggie?"

"Reggie? I'm not sure. Maybe, yes, oh it could have been, but I can't remember," the sister said, holding back tears.

"Then why didn't you just return it to Tamaya when you arrived?" Harold interjected. "Was it because you now knew it was valuable. Maybe you wanted to keep it; maybe you wanted to see if you could get more of these books. Maybe YOU and your sister conspired together to steal more, and when she got greedy, you KILLED HER!"

"Good Lord, stop it! No, no, that's not what happened!" Tisbe sobbed. "I forgot, I forgot I had the book! I love my sister; I love her!"

"Good try, Harold," charged Goldie. "But that theory doesn't fly; she didn't have a motive to off Norman or Ray."

"True," the opinionated man said and looked over at the pitiful woman who continued to sniffle. "But you have to admit I did a damn good job of cross-examining."

"Damn stupid," accused the lawyer. "More like an interrogation."

But for all that, the challenge was notably unsuccessful, and the sudden shifting of sentiments quickly changed to a more positive mood when Salisbury began to offer drinks. Wolfe, who now stationed himself by the mantle, mentally postulated what he was going to say. He was in no mood for chit chat and chastised himself for his part in what he considered a charade. He had a good mind to leave, yet, the stigma of being an ex-con offered him no other decision but to remain until the police could exonerate him.

"I will begin," said Harold. "That is if you all agree." He stood up and crossed the room, adding some ginger ale to his glass of whiskey. He felt lightheaded and wondered if perhaps he had been too hasty with his invitation to speak first.

"Madame," interrupted Salisbury. "I don't wish to be a killjoy; but I could use a bit of help in the kitchen."

"Help?" inquired the hostess.

"With the onions."

"Oh, I forgot," she acknowledged. "He's got allergies."

"To onions?" mocked Goldie.

"No, to the turnips."

"To the turnips," echoed Tisbe a bit amused.

"Yes, we keep the onions in the cellar with the turnips and other root vegetables," explained Ms. Rosebud.

"I see, so he needs someone to get the turnips?" inquired the sister.

"No, the onions," protested Wolfe with annoyance.

No one stirred. Distrust now dominated their lackluster dispositions. "Perhaps we all should venture to the cellar if no one is willing to take a risk," offered the lawyer.

"Maybe we can do without onions," Salisbury said. "However, my rice pilaf will not be the same without sautéed onions."

"The man is right; we need the onions. I'll go, but don't start without me," groaned Harold.

"We can't, you're starting first," reminded Tamaya with a slight shiver. "I need my sweater; I'm a bit chilly. Wolfe, would you be a dear and pour me a drink, light on the ice, and no ginger ale. I'll be back in a minute."

"Well, if we're all getting up, I need to powder my nose," quipped Goldie.

"And if everyone is leaving, I'm going to stretch my legs and return the book to the shelf," volunteered Tisbe.

There were now just two in the room, Peri Cason and Wolfe. "Forgive me for being so suspicious," the lawyer said. "It was not fair of me."

"Fair, I don't even know the meaning of the word anymore," Wolfe said dryly.

"No, you've had a time of it," the lawyer admitted.

They both sipped their drinks in silence; however, Wolfe felt no remorse for the dislike he felt for the woman. She was judgmental and boastful, a trait that he found more than loathsome. He moved away from the mantle and leaned against the wall where he could observe the whole room. Soon they would be reassembled, and she, Dr. Cason, would play the role she preferred, attorney. He gulped his drink and winced. "What the hell is keeping everyone?" he said.

There was a brisk shuffle of feet as Tisbe entered, looking frazzled. "Did you hear that!" she stuttered. "It sounded like something fell!"

"I don't hear anything," grimaced Wolfe.

"Me neither, but we've been in here waiting for everyone," reminded Miss Cason.

"Then, you're both deaf!" squawked Goldie. "I heard it too!" With her nose freshly powdered and her cheeks rouged, she resembled a kewpie doll. "Shhhh," she signaled. But there was nothing that seemed out of the ordinary. The old clock tapped a predictable beat, and the faint patter of rain had become routine.

Upstairs everything was quiet until the tap tap tap of Tamaya's cane moved down the stairs. She reached the bottom step and sighed. "I thought you went up for your sweater," Tisbe asked, inspecting the woman who sheepishly returned to her chair.

"I couldn't find it," remarked the woman, a bit out of breath. Mr. Wolfe handed her the whiskey and sat in the chair next to her. "Well, except for Harold, we're all accounted for."

"He's so damn persnickety, probably going through the onions as if he were choosing a date," joked Goldie conjuring up an image of the paunchy man examining the bulbs one by one. "He takes his food too damn seriously, kind of like you, Wolfe."

"Me, what the hell are you talking about?"

"Please, I can't think with all this arguing!" whined Tisbe.

"And what have you got to think about?" goaded Goldie.

"Oh, you are insufferable!" complained the sister. "I will be so happy to get out of this house!"

"Make that the two of us!" winked Goldie. "Finally, we can agree on something!"

"Did Mr. Harold return with the onions?" Picking a thread off his trousers, Salisbury paused by the doorway and then entered. His white apron remarkably well-pressed, and except for a tiny dab of olive oil, he was exceptionally neat.

Peri Cason slowly rose and, with wide eyes, approached the house-man. "He didn't come back up?"

"I didn't even know that he had gone to the cellar, and furthermore, I can't begin to saute without my onions," repeated Salisbury, this time addressing the hostess. "Time is critical, and when the oil is ready, then the onions must go in."

Tamaya tapped her fingers impatiently against the armrest. "Then, I suppose you should call down to him and ask him what's taking so long."

"Me, Madame?" However, by the look on her face, the house-man understood she was in one of her moods. "Of course, I will call down."

"Don't bother, Salisbury I'll go see what the old boy is up to," Goldie volunteered.

"If you will follow me, Ms. Hildebrandt, I will take you to the cellar stairwell." And as he glided away, the old woman trailed behind muttering a shameful bit of expletives.

* * *

The eye of the lighthouse appears at night like a nocturnal animal. Reggie completed his watch and waited for his father to came up with his snack. "Looks like the weather is going to clear soon," Reggie exclaimed. Jay set the cornbread and milk on the workbench and sat down on the edge of the cot. He turned to his son and shook his head.

"Are we looking at the same horizon?"

Reggie stood up and leaned lightly against the pane. The signal beam was on a new rotation as he turned to his father. "I can't see it."

"Precisely, neither do I."

"Oh," the boy said and sat back down, reaching for his bread. "When will you take the ferry back out?"

"When I can see the horizon."

\* \* \*

"He's not there!"

"Not there?" repeated Salisbury.

"That's what I said; he's not in the cellar." Goldie closed the door behind her and took no time in citing her disgust. "Too damn stuffy in that stairwell! I called down to him, but all I got back was my echo."

"Oh, then I wonder where my onions are," mumbled the houseman.

"Hell if I know!"

"Well, my rice pilaf will not be quite as good without them. But I suppose I could substitute onions with a few shallots," he said.

"Why don't you just do that while I go in and let the rest know that Harold is missing!" she gripped.

"Oh, I doubt he is missing, Madame."

"Well then, maybe we just misplaced him!" Goldie suggested, and walking away, turned back into the library. "He's not there," Goldie announced.

"Not in the cellar?" Tisbe fretted.

"Nope, and he's too big to lose, which means he either left the premises or never made it downstairs."

"Oh that wily son-of-a-gun, I bet he left. I bet he left!" fumed Wolfe.

"I doubt it," remarked the hostess. "Unless he had a cab or coach, he would never have walked. Mark my words, he will turn up," noted the hostess with authority.

"She's right, he's not the type to walk very far," agreed Peri Cason. "As soon as it's dinnertime, he'll come out from his hiding place like a hungry puppy."

For the first time in several days, there was laughter. Even Wolfe cracked a smile at the notion of Harold Dover retreating from behind the sofa. For several minutes each guest delighted in offering their rendition of where the pompous man might hold-up: the bathroom, the bedroom, even in the cupboard. Still, no one mentioned that he actually could be in trouble. The perceivable conclusion might have crossed their minds, but they were having too much fun at his expense to ruin their amusement. The noisy room resumed their mockery with cartoonish imitations and lampooning the boorish man; up until Tisbe, shrouded in fear, flitted down the stairs.

"Oh my heavens, oh dear, my heart cannot take anymore!" she moaned and stumbled down the last few steps. Wolfe was the first to see the spinster trip and helped her to her feet. But before he could ask what had happened, the dread on her face imparted all the words needed to know something was wrong.

"What is it? What has happened," cried Ms. Rosebud.

"It's Harold," Tisbe moaned, "he's had an accident! I tried to help him, but he's so, so.."

"So what, woman, damn it, tell us, so what?" demanded Wolfe.

"I think he's…"

"Dead?" questioned Wolfe.

"Yes, oh, it's so horrible!" said Tisbe in an agitated whisper.

But as the word *dead* fell from the trembling woman's lips, Peri Cason's gasp deepened into a groan of disbelief. She ran down the hallway and then stopped at the rear staircase that led to the cellar.

The door was open wide enough to see Harold Dover face down in the stairwell surrounded by onions. "He must have tripped coming up! Those damn things are everywhere!" Peri announced as she tossed an onion over the balcony.

"He was only supposed to get one," explained Tamaya who had followed behind. "My poor dear, Harold." She glared at the man and poked him with her cane. "Oh, dear, I believe Harold is gone."

There was now a gathering at the open doorway. Goldie, Tisbe, Wolfe, Peri, and Salisbury, who too had heard the commotion, gathered around and leaned over one another to get a good look at the large fellow.

"I suppose you want me to take him to the wine cellar, Madame." The butler exhaled an exasperated sigh after he spoke.

"That would be very good, Salisbury. Perhaps by way of these back stairs," she said, pointing at the open doorway.

"If I could just get a few of these onions first," he said, and excusing himself from the others, proceeded to gather an apronful.

"For heaven's sake!" Peri groaned. "How can you think of food at a time like this? We have another dead body, and for all we know, he was murdered!"

"Oh, don't be such an old fogey," snarled Goldie. "Salisbury is only thinking of us! Besides, he doesn't look murdered to me!"

"And since when are you an expert on murder?"

"I never said I was; it just seems obvious that a runaway onion killed him!" Goldie pointed out.

"If you don't mind, Mr. Wolfe, as soon as I put these in the kitchen, I could use your assistance taking Mr. Harold to the cooler," petitioned Salisbury.

"And then we will eat," announced the hostess. "In the meantime, ladies, join me in a glass of port. I know that's what Harold would want us to do."

After what seemed to be the better part of an hour, Mr. Wolfe rejoined the guests. "Well, we better find out who's the killer, or we'll run out of room in the wine cellar," laughed Wolfe morbidly. He handed Tamaya two bottles of Chablis. "We had to make space for Harold's arms, so I figured we could all take one for the team."

"I'm still not convinced the killer is anyone here," Tamaya said confidently. She placed the wine bottles on the dinner table and escorted the four remaining guests to their seats. "I've hosted many parties and let it be known; no one has ever left unhappy."

"Or dead?" asked Wolfe.

"Well, no, not dead. Maybe a bit tipsy, but dead, never." She gestured for everyone to take their seats and then leaned her cane against the table. "I hope everyone is hungry," and with a forced smile, she sat down.

Salisbury entered and glided about as if on air. "I believe Mr. Harold left this behind," he said and handed a small-caliber pistol to the hostess. "It must have fallen from his person when he fell."

"Well, that settles it, my dear Harold wasn't the killer, or else he would have used this on one of us," claimed Tamaya placing the weapon on her lap.

"Or perhaps he was the killer and just didn't have time to use it," snapped Goldie.

"Don't you think you better get rid of the gun?" Peri asked warily.

"Allow me, Madame, I can put it here," Salisbury suggested, and with a look of glee, Tamaya handily handed over the pistol. All eyes turned to the buffet where it was placed under the lid of the soup tureen.

"Well, now that that's out of the way, we can proceed. A toast! What shall we toast to?" Ms. Rosebud asked and lifted her glass towards the chandelier.

"To the last man or woman standing," teased Tisbe.

"My, my, you have a sense of humor," goaded Wolfe to the sister. "A new side?"

"Not really. With Harold in the wine cellar, I can safely say I am vindicated of any wrongdoing. After all, I was the last one who wanted to take the deal. And with him gone, there is no deal. So, you see, I have no motive."

"To the last one standing!" chanted the guests, all except Peri, who was preoccupied with the sister's last remark. As soon as the glasses were set back on the table, Salisbury busied himself with refills and opening more Chablis.

"You have a good point," Peri acknowledged.

Ms. Rosebud, who had already finished her second glass of Chablis, was leaning over her plate, picking at the shallots. "You know," she exclaimed, taking another bite, "Salisbury is quite correct. His rice pilaf is better with onions."

# CHAPTER 12

PERI Cason opened her notebook to a new page and began to scribble. Her wit was about to be tested. The gun was in the soup tureen, Tisbe was too naïve to be a probable suspect, which left Wolfe, Goldie, Tamaya, and Salisbury. The houseman was the wild card. She tapped her pencil against the pad and stared at the portrait hanging next to the dresser. It was a painting of a dog. She screwed her nose up at the canine; she disliked dogs ever since she had been nipped at by her aunt's Pekingese years ago. A spirit of the unpleasant memory took hold of the woman when a faint knock on the door quickly disbanded her daydream. Cason looked at her watch; it was past eleven. She hesitated and scrambled to find something she could use to defend herself. If need be, she'd throw the desk chair at the intruder. The knock came again, louder this time. "Just a minute." She swung her legs over the side of the bed and cracked open the door. It was Tisbe, dressed in a high collar pink dressing gown and house slippers. Cason pulled open the door wider.

"I haven't woken you, have I?" the sister asked.

"No," said the lawyer, still clutching the doorknob, "I was just working."

"I know it's late, but I wanted to bring this to you." The woman handed her a cup of warm milk. "I saw the light under the door and thought maybe you could use this to help you sleep," she said.

Peri looked at the tray and smiled. "This takes me back to when I was a little girl. I haven't had warm milk in ages."

"It's even better now," Tisbe said, garnishing a smile. "I just thought you might enjoy it more with a drop of whiskey. I helped myself to a cup too."

Peri lifted the saucer. "I'll take mine in my room, thanks."

"Me too, in my room," the woman whispered and giggled like a schoolgirl. "Sweet dreams!"

Peri stood in the doorway and watched as Tisbe finagled both the bedroom key and the tray of milk. It took a bit of maneuvering, but in a moment, she shuffled into her room. The lawyer peered at her cup and frowned, closing the door behind her. "Ugh," she thought. "A perfectly good cup of whiskey ruined by milk," she muttered under her breath and immediately poured it into the potted plant.

\* \* \*

It was past nine o'clock when Tamaya woke up. Salisbury was standing over her bed with a pot of tea. "Madame, I believe we have a problem," he announced. He set the tea service on the bureau and gently fluffed her pillows as she sat up.

"Thank you, Salisbury." He handed her the teacup and waited as she took a sip. "Now, what is this about a problem. It's not the onions again, I hope."

"No, Madame, we are in ample supply of root vegetables. It is Miss Tisbe. It appears that Miss Cason has been knocking on her door, and she doesn't answer."

"Perhaps the woman is asleep," replied Tamaya, airing annoyance by the early morning's announcement.

"That's what I said, but Miss Cason bleated something about a potted plant. She is quite upset with the Schefflera; it seems that overnight it has wilted." Tamaya said nothing and signaled for another bit of her tea. Salisbury filled the cup and stared at her indifferently as she lingered over her second cup.

"Have the rest of the guests had their breakfasts?" the hostess asked, offering back the empty teacup.

"Yes, Madame. Presently, Mrs. Hildebrandt and Mr. Wolfe have settled in the library and are arguing over a game of chess. It's just Miss Cason that seems to be more than a bit out of sorts."

"Please tell her that I will be down shortly, and we will get her another plant. I believe one of the palms from the veranda will do."

"Certainly, Madame, a potted palm from the veranda, up the stairs, and down the hall into Miss Cason's chamber," he said with an unsettling voice.

"Don't bother!" exclaimed Peri Cason at the open door.

"Why we were just talking about you, you must have a sixth sense." Tamaya Rosebud waved her hand, feverishly gesturing for her friend to enter.

"For crying out loud, Tamaya! I don't give a damn about getting another plant. But I am worried about Tisbe. She won't answer her door."

"Maybe she's sleeping or took a sleeping pill. You know how they affect some people," the hostess said, dismissing any notion of trouble.

"No, no, I think there's a problem. And if you don't mind, I believe we should immediately break down the door."

"Break down the door, Madame?" remarked the butler, believing his contribution to the conversation was now quite necessary.

"Yes, Salisbury," demanded Peri, "break down the damn door."

"Wouldn't it just be better to use a key?" he asked, and placing his hand into his pocket, removed a small ring of brass keys.

"I agree, Peri, I believe breaking down a perfectly intact oak door would be a bit extreme," the hostess nodded, and then with a flick of her wrist, motioned for Salisbury to go and unlock the door. "But be sure to knock first!" she called.

"Naturally, Madame," he answered.

But determined to get to the bottom of things, Peri disregarded her friend and followed behind Salisbury while he rapped ever so gently on the locked door. After a moment's silence, he shrugged his shoulders and tried again. Still, there was no response, at which point he tired several of the keys until he found what he believed to be the correct one. However, to his dismay, the lock resisted. He shimmied the latch, but it remained steadfast. He wiped the key against his shirtsleeve and placed it back into the lock. "It certainly is not being cooperative," he lamented.

"Here, let me try," clamored the impatient woman, and pushing the houseman aside, she wiggled the key and the knob at the same time. The tumblers rattled, and at last, the door released its hold. But it was Salisbury who entered first and Salisbury that first discovered the old sister in bed. Tiptoeing lightly, he stood over the bed, reached forward, and gently shook the barefoot. He waited for a moment and then shook more vigorously. "Miss Tisbe, can you hear me?" he asked in a bold voice, and with a deadpan tone, declared, "I believe she's dead."

"Dead?" screamed Peri Cason, running from the room. "Oh, my Lord, she's dead!"

"Who's dead!" screamed Goldie from downstairs.

"Tisbe, she's dead!" cried the lawyer, now charging down the stairs. "Someone poisoned her, someone killed Tisbe, and they tried to kill me too!"

"What, Tisbe, poisoned?" exclaimed Mr. Wolfe getting up from the chessboard.

"Where do you think you're going, Wolfe? We're not finished, and I'm just about to take your queen!" grumbled Goldie.

"Be right back, and don't cheat!" he said, and as he hurried out of the library, he met Tamaya Rosebud coming down the stairs.

"It's Peri; she appears to be quite upset. Something about a plant," the hostess explained, lifting her white cane in the direction of the dining room. Wolfe followed the neck of the stick, leading him to the threshold. However, as he stepped through, he sensed something was not right. The silhouette of a woman aiming a gun appeared from behind the drapes.

"Don't come any closer, Wolfe. I'll shoot if I have to."

"Where'd you get that thing?" he asked, trying to remain undaunted by the firearm.

"From the tureen, the soup tureen, and I'm not afraid to use it. Just step away, Wolfe."

"What's wrong with you, Cason?" Hoping she'd put the gun down, he slowly walked towards her with open hands.

"Not a damn thing, I'm leaving, and you can't stop me. Just move, move the hell away and open the front door." Pointing with the pistol, she directed him to step forward. He followed her command, and warily made his way into the foyer.

"Where are you going, Peri?" Tamaya asked. "You haven't had your coffee. Come, Dear, let's go into the kitchen and have Salisbury fix us some."

"You're batty!" Peri announced. "You're out of your mind, Tamaya! I'm not going to stay another minute in this nuthouse. Unbolt the door, Wolfe!" Fresh air and sunlight rolled in as he pulled open the front door.

"Oh my, look, everyone, the sun, now isn't that nice!" declared Ms. Rosebud leaning against her cane. "You know, we can have our breakfast on the veranda, Dear!" she called out. But the distraught lawyer did not answer her. Peri Cason scrambled out of the house and down the driveway, still with gun in hand. Looking ahead past the trees, she fled as fast as her legs would carry her, and though not built for speed, she was making excellent progress despite her limitations.

\* \* \*

Peri Cason arrived at the Drunken Mermaid breathless and shaken. The usual cluster of patrons was enjoying the day. Mr. Lee sat at the end of the bar, concealed by the exotic dragon head when the lawyer entered. She arrived without fanfare; however, her presence aroused the entire tavern. It was the gun, and without thinking, she flung open the door with the pistol by her side. Such a sight is often not well-received. "Let me have a gin and tonic," she said and hoisted herself up on the stool. She was tired and without care to her surroundings; she released a staccato of indiscernible mumbles.

The barkeep gestured to Mr. Lee, who slid snakelike to the back of the tavern, where he whispered a few words to the two men sitting at a table. And then he slithered back to watch the woman. "House label, okay?" the bartender asked. Peri nodded and placed her head on the bar, resting it against the hand still holding the gun. The bartender made no moves and kept his eyes on the woman as he squeezed lime into her drink. He tried not to appear nervous and placed the glass on a napkin. Peri lifted her head, and with her left hand, reached for the drink when suddenly she felt the breath of someone leaning over her.

"I don't know who you are, lady, but you better have a damn good reason for bringing that gun in here." His voice trudged calmly from his mouth to her ears. Slowly she twisted her neck and fixed her eyes on a black wire mustache and a head covered in grey hair half-hidden beneath a wool cap. His words resonated in her mind. She was thirsty and tired and frightened, a deadly combination for a woman with a weapon. "Where you from, lady?" the man asked.

"That's curious," she thought. "He didn't ask for my name." She sat up, her right hand still on the pistol, and raising the left one, took a sip of her drink. "I was a guest at the Rosebud house. But there's been trouble there."

"Trouble?" pressed the man soliciting information. "What kind of trouble?" He towered over her, keeping an eye on the pistol as he spoke.

"Bad trouble," she repeated. She didn't court trouble, but in that instant, something in her head popped. An invisible lattice of distrust was conjuring up fear. Her lips hung apart, quivering as she put forth a lifeless whine. "Murder, there have been several murders," she revealed.

Mr. Lee's ears perked up as he moved from his barstool to an earshot of the conversation. He focused on the woman, not the gun, and wondered if she could be trusted.

"What do you mean murder?" the man asked more emphatically.

To be confronted by such a question was not unreasonable; however, it was its harsh delivery that sparked the frightened lawyer's agitation, and she glared at him with the look of a scared animal. "Who are you?" she demanded.

"Trigg, Mort Trigg. I'm the sheriff."

A calm fell over the woman as she suddenly became revived like a drooping lily takes to water. "Sheriff?" She relaxed and then took another sip. "Well, Sheriff Rigg…"

"Trigg, with a T," he corrected.

"Well, Trigg, I'm Peri Cason, and I'm going to tell you there are quite a few dead bodies at that house."

The lawman watched as the woman finished her drink, and covertly slid the gun to her lap. But however innocent a move it was, it was not taken as such by the Sheriff. And thinking that his life was in jeopardy, he reached for her weapon. "No," screamed the woman, "no!"

And as he tried to seize it, Mr. Lee jumped up from his stool and yelled, "Take that evil woman!" Dismissing any idea of innocence, the fortune teller shoved Cason from behind, throwing her off balance. A shot was fired, and in a matter of seconds, Peri Cason lay between the feet of both men.

Blood trickled on the floor as the Sheriff kicked the fired weapon away with his foot. "Hell of a stupid way to go, getting shot by your own gun." He knelt over the woman and turned his eyes upward. "You saved my ass, Lee," he said to the patron. "Saved my mangy ass."

# CHAPTER 13

"Finally, a lovely day. Too bad the others couldn't be around to enjoy the sun," Tamaya announced, feeling distinctly at ease. The grey clouds had slipped past, and like yards of unfurled canvas, the sky was blue again. Favorable weather extinguished all ill feelings, and as the remaining guests sat on the veranda, Salisbury passed around a tray of deviled eggs and tea sandwiches.

"That Trigg isn't so bad for a Sheriff," Goldie remarked.

"Monte; he's always been a good friend." Tamaya's faraway look needed further investigation.

"Not a bad guy, is that code?" Goldie hinted. "Cause in my book, sister; he's more than 'a good guy' kind of relationship." She hoped she had provoked the hostess into confessing some juicy tidbits.

Tamaya smiled but wouldn't take the bait and decided not to enter into a discussion about her past. "He's a friend, just a good friend," she continued.

"Well, friend or not, the fact that he didn't bother us with a lot of snooping around makes him a first-rate guy. The last thing I need is a cop on my tail," Wolfe said, inserting his two cents into the conversation. He was more than happy; he was relieved.

"Too bad for Peri, taking the entire wrap," Tamaya lamented. "Such a shame."

"What wrap? The cops thought she was a crazy broad with crazy ideas, not too farfetched if you ask me. The only one we needed to corroborate was Harold. But, since the police decided to list him as missing, it all ended up just the way it should, with us in the clear. I still think your friend Trigg thinks Peri killed him." Goldie leaned back in her chaise lounge and sucked her lemonade through a straw.

"You know, Madame, you still haven't found out who the killer is." Salisbury liked to stir up things, and today was no different.

"As usual, you're right, Salisbury," Tamaya sighed. "I suppose before you two leave, we need to find out." Her eyes met her guests with mixed emotions.

Goldie shaded her hand across her brow. She sat up in the lounge and slurped her drink until nothing more could be drained from the glass. "Nervous?" Wolfe whispered and grinned.

"No, I'm not nervous, are you?" she said, trying to antagonize him with her acid tone. He winked and then leaned back in his chaise.

"If I didn't know better, I'd believe you and Wolfe had conspired together," Tamaya said with a suggestive laugh.

"And what about you and old Salisbury here, he seems more than your houseman," Goldie added. This time it was Ms. Rosebud who winked.

"We could just blame it all on Miss Peri and get on with our lives," Salisbury suggested. He felt emboldened and decided to join in the discussion. After all, if anyone accused him, he had a right to defend himself.

There was a thoughtful pause, but a unanimous agreement that such a verdict would leave everyone quite unsatisfied. No, they decided. It was imperative to arrive at a resolution, or it would be like a cheap ending to a great book. And no one enjoys that kind of conclusion.

"Now that they're gone, we need to utilize what's left of our time together. I certainly will not be returning," Wolfe admitted.

"Me neither, as soon as I get back to my nice quiet cottage I'm staying put for a long time," Goldie said. "I've had enough fun for a while."

A flock of sparrows flew overhead, forming a shadow. They circled the sky and settled on the hillside to feed on the turned-up insects the storm had disturbed. No one seemed to be in a hurry to talk, so they watched the birds until a sudden gust sent them airborne again.

"Well, we can't just sit here as if nothing happened," announced Goldie. "I say we make a pact. Whatever we say between us can never be revealed to anyone. If one of us goes down, we all go down."

The scheme was hard to dispute, stifling any reluctance to band together. Ms. Rosebud laughed richly, sanctioning the idea with a resounding, "Splendid!"

"Good, then let's drink on it," Goldie asserted. "We'll take an oath of allegiance that can't be broken."

"So melodramatic," complained Wolfe. "As far as I'm concerned, a handshake is more than sufficient." However, they ignored his gripe and took an oath of secrecy, followed by a customary stiff shot of whiskey. After which, it was declared binding.

"We'll begin with Ray," Goldie decided. "Fess up, who killed him?"

"Certainly not I," Salisbury exclaimed. "I found the little man quite annoying, but not enough to take his life."

"Nope, not me," said Wolfe. "Knew him back in the old days, and he never did any harm to me."

"I found him quite amusing, in a crude sort of way," Tamaya said. "And as for his story, well, he certainly was tricked by that Miller and the daughter. He had a difficult time of it. I rather felt sorry for him, too trusting." All eyes turned to Goldie.

"What, what are you staring at?" she asked with a poker face. "Why would I hurt Ray, we were good friends." But the more they stared, the harder it was to keep a straight face. "Okay, I admit it. But he was going to ruin everything. He wanted to take the deal, and if that happened, I'd lose everything. I'm a single woman on a pension, and the book is my only other means of income. If he had gone along with us, nothing would have happened."

"So, you killed him?" Tamaya asked.

"Well, if you put it like that, it was a sort of accident. No, maybe more of a dare. He was stupid enough to let me put the ascot around his neck."

"My ascot!" snarled Wolfe.

"Well, I certainly couldn't use my sash."

"Lord, Goldie, I'll never be able to wear that red ascot again!" Wolfe complained.

"Okay, now that you know, what about Javotte? That's one bitch I didn't touch," Goldie swore. "Didn't like her but didn't lay a hand on her."

"I wouldn't have hurt her either," Wolfe announced. "I didn't like the idea that she wanted to take the deal, but no, it wasn't me."

"Pass," said Salisbury. "I liked her. She was very complimentary about my cooking and a great help in the kitchen."

"So are we to conclude that aside from Goldie, there was another killer in our midst?" Tamaya asked with surprise.

"Yeah, and if I were going to offer my calculations, and I am usually right, I'd say it was you, Ms. Rosebud!" Goldie shouted.

"Me? What motive would I have to take the life of that dear, simple woman."

"Because you're sweet on Mr. Jay, that's why," announced the houseman.

"Salisbury! Such an accusation," the hostess clamored and placing her hand over her mouth, she feigned disappointment.

"So sorry, Madame, but I see the way you look at him," Salisbury jested.

"Ohhhh," exclaimed Wolfe. "That makes sense; you were jealous!"

"Jealous enough to poison Jay, too?" asked Goldie.

"Heavens, no. He just happened not to be able to tolerate strawberries. That was none of my doing."

"Okay, spill!" Goldie said and sipped her freshened glass of whiskey with extra enjoyment. "This I gotta hear."

"Although it was dark during the séance, there was just enough light to see under the table where that floozy was playing footsy with Jay. It was all I could do to control my temper. Then, as luck would have it, the planchette flew off the board and accidentally hit her temple. I instantly knew it wouldn't have enough clout to have caused any real harm except to give her a nasty bruise. So, I helped it along with my cane. I gave her a good whack on the side of the head. You must believe me; I only meant to give her a bit of a headache."

"I'll say, one hell of a headache!" noted Wolfe.

"So that's when the tip of that stick got discolored," Goldie said. "Good thing the police didn't analyze it for blood."

"Sorry, Madame, but the secret about Mr. Jay would have come out eventually."

"Oh shut up, Salisbury," Tamaya sulked. "And pour me another drink!"

"Of course, Madame."

"So that makes two, and only three to go." Goldie felt exonerated from her guilt now that she knew about Tamaya.

"This is quite extraordinary," remarked Tamaya sipping her drink. "All this time, everyone thought there was just one culprit, and here we have two."

"Make that three, Madame."

"You, Salisbury?" questioned the hostess taking note of the house-man's sullen mood.

"I am afraid so," he admitted, and placing the bottle of whiskey to his lips, he swallowed what was left. Then he dabbed his mouth on the napkin and looked for a place to sit. Ms. Rosebud shifted her feet aside and tapped the chaise, where he plopped down with the bottle resting between his legs.

"Oh, cheer up, once you get it off your chest, you'll feel so much better. I know I do!" replied Goldie with a bit too much glee by some-one who had just admitted to a murder.

Salisbury nodded and sighed heavily as if the burden of the world was on his shoulders and his alone. "It was I who spiked the whiskey," he professed. "I didn't mean to kill anyone, just put them to sleep."

"I'll say," remarked Wolfe. "Not this stuff, I hope!" he growled.

"Oh, no. It was last evening's nightcap Miss Tisbe made for herself and Miss Peri. They were forever making such a chatter, idle gossip; all I wanted was a good night's rest." The houseman looked up with remorse; however, no one believed his pathetic excuse.

"Come on, Salisbury," Tamaya said. "Didn't you really know how much sedative you added?"

"Actually, no, Madame, it always works on you." Salisbury pulled the cork from the bottle and tipped it back into his mouth. A few drops slithered down the side and into his throat.

"Oh, for heaven's sake, take that out of your mouth and stop sulking," scolded Goldie. "So let's see, that makes three." She reached over and gave Wolfe a shove with her elbow. "Your turn."

A gathering of clouds had gathered overhead, and the sun that only minutes ago was shining upon the veranda had retreated. Mr. Wolfe put his finger in his drink and stirred it around. He could feel the attention shift towards him, and although he objected to joining into this game, he began to feel himself cave. "How do I know that one of you won't turn us all in?"

"You don't," remarked Ms. Rosebud. "However, why would we. Two bodies and two confessions remain unaccounted for. As a result, one of us must be the murderer, or as in Salisbury's case, the accidental murderer."

"Which I'm not buyin," remarked Goldie coldly.

Mr. Wolfe finished his drink. "I'll pass."

"Pass, you can't pass, we made a pact!" screamed Goldie tipping her eyeglasses over her nose. "And if you do pass, then we'll assume you offed Harold and Norman. You don't want two murders on your conscience, do you?"

"If it makes you feel any more in the mood to confess, I saw you," said Salisbury.

"What! You saw me; you saw me do what?" demanded Wolfe. He glared at the houseman as if possessed.

"I saw you go outside with the trash."

"And what does that mean?"

"It means," said Goldie, "that you were in the same place where we found Norman dead. I was wondering how the big guy could have fallen."

"If you saw me, then why didn't you speak up?" Wolfe prodded.

"Because, Sir, I had no proof that you were the perpetrator of the crime. But, by bringing it up now, it appears that you have incriminated yourself." Salisbury smiled wilily.

"Poor Norman," sighed Tamaya shaking her head with regret. She flashed an image in her mind of the large man and sighed loudly again.

"Oh, don't poor Norman me!" cried Wolfe. "The man was a two-bit thief. When I accidentally met up with him by the trash bins, he was all ready to take the deal, perfectly content to change sides against Goldie and me. He was a greedy bastard. With Ray and Javotte out of the way, he said nothing was stopping him from getting more. That's when things got heated. He pushed, I shoved, and as the story goes, things got a bit rough. That's when my second shove knocked him down."

"So, you're trying to tell us this was another accident," Goldie remarked.

"No, this was no accident. It was him or me." Wolfe looked around the veranda and then stood up. His legs were shaky, and he brushed his hair back with his hand. "Let's get us another bottle, Salisbury. Anyone else needs a drink?"

\* \* \*

They followed Salisbury into the library, where he liberated the corkscrew from the bar and waved it above his head. "To the last one standing!" he joked, and having drunk a bit too much, he was feeling more like a guest than a houseman.

"Oh, my, perhaps you should lie down," Ms. Rosebud suggested after the butler began to take on a shade of green. "You look positively awful," she said.

"Yes, Madame, I believe you're correct. If you will excuse me, I think I will follow your wise instructions." Like a teenager after his first drink, Salisbury stumbled, hanging on to the furniture until he reached the threshold. Rather than gliding, he appeared to skate, poorly that is until he opened the door leading downstairs to his quarters. "I'm okay!" he shouted, and in the next few minutes, the rest of the party-goers could hear the slow retreat downward.

"He could never hold his liquor," remarked Tamaya. "He'll sleep it off and then act as if nothing in the world happened."

"Nothing did happen," said Wolfe.

"Nothing except three confessions to murders and death by accidental poisoning," Goldie reminded him. "We do have the matter of Harold; anyone want to take a swipe?"

"Oh, yes, Harold. Well, he'll be missed, so we had better come up with a decent excuse for his departure," Tamaya said. "I suppose I could tell the office he never arrived. But no, Harold was such a stickler for detail, he most likely called his secretary." She set her cane against the chair and sat down. "You know, I could just say nothing." Both Goldie and Wolfe looked at each other for a cue to speak, but neither had anything to say. "If anyone comes around, I'll just tell them he left without saying goodbye."

"And no one would find that irregular?" Wolfe asked, feeling as though her suggestion was filled with holes.

"Oh, I don't know, let someone prove it wasn't true." Ms. Rosebud was tired and wished for the entire event to go away. All she wanted to do was to be left alone.

"She's got a point, Wolfe. Except for one minor detail. What the hell are you going to do with everyone still in the wine cellar?" Goldie asked, turning to Tamaya.

"Since no one seems to want them, Trigg said I could put them in the crypt." She pointed to the window. "Didn't you see the family cemetery? Would you like to go outside and see it?" Tamaya was quite willing to take them. "It's such a lovely day; I could show you around."

"No, that's alright, I'll take your word for it. Anyway, we never got to the heart of the last matter." Mr. Wolfe walked over to the window and pulled the drapes so he could look outside. An ornate, marble structure appeared in the distance. He flinched and then shut the curtain.

"Yeh, who did in Harold? Want to take bets?" Goldie snickered.

"Well, unless it was one of us, we'll never know," Tamaya sighed.

Goldie was pacing the floor, leaving a ring of footprints in the soft rug as she spoke. "Except, there must be a clue we've overlooked. We know who it couldn't be because they're dead. And we know that

Harold was coming up from the cellar with a bunch of onions. He took the back stairwell, which was dark, so he most likely tripped."

"Did anyone look in the cellar after he was pronounced dead?" asked Wolfe.

"An obvious faux-pas!" exclaimed Goldie. "Only, if the killer was in the cellar, then how did he or she escape? I say we go in through the back entrance and look around. Tamaya, check out the top of the rear hallway stairs and look around where Dover fell."

"You know, if one of us is the killer, it will save us a hell of a lot of trouble to just confess," Wolfe remarked. He was too comfortable and wanted nothing to do with moving. But to his disappointment, neither woman admitted to the crime. "Damn, okay, okay, but Goldie, this is the last thing I want to do!"

* * *

The vegetables are stored in the root cellar, a dark, spacious room of stone walls, dirt floor, and wooden bins. Its subterranean location usually weathered a storm; however, this had been no ordinary storm. The continuous rain saturated the ground beneath the house, and as the earth became gorged, the water that could not be absorbed in the bedrock drew upward. Goldie held on to the handrail behind Wolfe. From the bottom steps, they could see the floor of the root cellar. Embedded in the mud were footprints, a man's footprints which headed in one direction from the stairwell to the vegetable bin and back again. "Doesn't look like anything is out of sorts," said Goldie. A reluctancy to step into the mud with her newly polished shoes held her back from proceeding further.

Wolfe remained skeptical and observed the room and, with his keen vision, assembled a more analytic observation. "I can see from here that the prints were all made from one pair of shoes. No reason to get into the muck of things," he laughed, noting his pun. "Yes, indeed. We can without reservations confirm Harold Dover was alone when he collected the onions."

"Unless someone had the exact same size and shoe," Goldie added.

"True, but highly unlikely," he remarked with an air of authority.

Goldie glanced down at Wolfe's feet and whistled. "Well, Sasquatch, you have nothing to worry about!"

Tamaya Rosebud tugged on the cord dangling in the upstairs' stairwell, but no light came on. It wasn't until she flipped on the hallway switch that she was in full sight of her disgust. "My lovely wooden stairs!" she exclaimed, and with her cane poked the muddy footprints.

\* \* \*

Salisbury had removed a pan of scones from the oven and was feverously slicing lemons when he heard a knock on the door. His neatly starched uniform had been pressed, as usual, to perfection, over which he wore a red and white apron. "Can someone get that?" he called with tempered annoyance.

Goldie opened the door for the seaman, who was trailed by a beam of sunlight. "I've come by report some good news. The ferry is up and running, and anytime you wish to leave, we can call the coach to retrieve you and your belongings," the man said. Sporting a day-old beard, he looked even more like the part of a lighthouse keeper.

"Finally," scowled Goldie. "Well, come on in, I'm sure Tamaya will be glad to see you," goaded the old woman remembering the hostess's confession. The house had a distinct smell of baked goods that wafted from the kitchen into the library where Mr. Wolfe and Tamaya were enjoying the peace of the afternoon. "Here Jay, sit next to Tamaya," insisted Goldie, and watching the librarian's face, she thought she saw a grin of approval.

The old skipper took off his cap and set it on his lap. "So, what's this about the ferry," asked Wolfe. "I was hoping I could finally get out of here, no offense to you, Ms. Rosebud."

"None taken," the woman said.

"Yep, looks like Reggie got the ferry going this morning. I'll be taking her out in about an hour. Figure I can make at least two more runs before nightfall."

"I can be packed in less than a half-hour," exclaimed Goldie. Her enthusiasm only rivaled Tamaya Rosebud, who was more than ready to rid herself of the two guests.

"Me, fifteen minutes, that's all I need," Mr. Wolfe announced.

"Before tea?" asked Tamaya, now a bit sorry that she had secretly wished her guests away. The sound of her lament gave way for the two guests to reconsider her request.

"Okay, one cup and a scone, and then we gotta get going!" Goldie agreed.

There was a soft patter across the floor as Salisbury entered. "Tea, Madame," he proposed, but as he set the tray on the table, the hostess expelled a sudden gasp followed by a disparaging look.

"What is it?" Mr. Jay asked, noticing Ms. Rosebud's expression turn from sweet-tempered to sour.

"Salisbury, your shoes!" she exclaimed. A path of dried mud had followed the houseman into the library.

"Nothing that can't be cleaned up with a brush and dustpan, Madame," Salisbury said, and with a slight smirk, he bent down and took off his shoes. Standing in yellow stocking feet, he went on with his business as if nothing happened.

"You don't suppose you're thinking what I'm thinking?" Goldie whispered, leaning over to Wolfe. She found herself watching the man as he glided about the room serving tea.

Wolfe sighed and smiled widely. "Well, not to sound trite, but perhaps this time, the butler did it."